Moonveil Saga

Volume 1

Kristen Ling

Illustrated by
月夜野・りあ

Moonveil Saga

EMORY HOUSE PUBLISHING

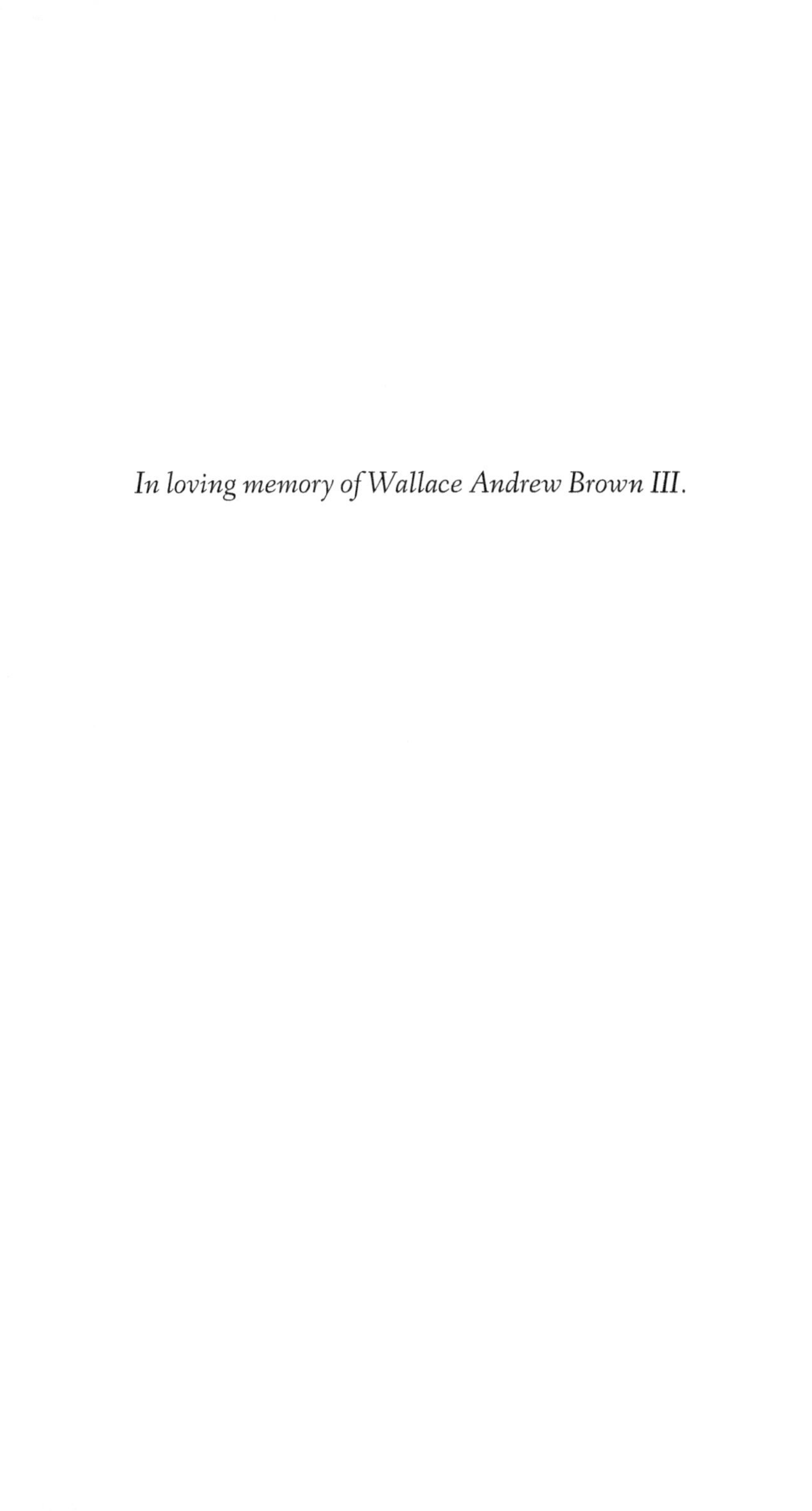

In loving memory of Wallace Andrew Brown III.

Disclaimer

This book is intended for readers **18 and up.**

Prologue

VEILKEEPER

A Veilkeeper maintains and protects the boundary between the Apparition World—also known as the Demon World—and the Physical World, often called the Human World.

Demons, extraterrestrials, and wandering spirits exist across Earth, the stars, the cosmos, and beyond.

The role is simple in theory: locate and capture—or destroy—anything that threatens the living world.

Veilkeepers are never chosen at random. They carry a rare, specific energy. Their identities are kept secret.

The rulers of the Spirit World oversee their discovery and training. But there's one unbreakable rule: if a Veilkeeper turns their back on their duty or uses their power for selfish gain, they'll be executed.

No trial. No second chances. Their power will be reborn in someone else.

There are currently **three Veilkeepers** living on Earth.

Chapter One
Aurelius

It hasn't always been easy. The process by which the Spirit World decides to awaken each Veilkeeper is complex. The first part of that process is finding them—which can sometimes take years.

How do we find them? We listen. We search for unusually exceptional human beings walking among the ordinary. For example, one keeper, decades ago, wasn't discovered until he was in his early eighties, while another was found when he was only eight years old. It's difficult—like searching for a needle in a haystack.

To make matters worse, we can only confirm their status as Veilkeepers during a full moon. Their aura glows only under its light. Why this happens, I don't know. I've asked my father countless times, but he never gives an answer.

My father is King Aurelius Sr., and I am his son, Prince Aurelius Jr.—or Auri, as my Veilkeepers call me.

My father leaves the task of handling Veilkeepers to me. My duty is to find them and guide them to where they are needed to protect the living world. It has always been this way.

The past century has been interesting. My job was fairly easy for the first half of it, as I only had one Veil-keeper to manage—Kosei.

Kosei "awakened," as we call it, when he was seventeen years old. I found him while he was defending a homeless man one night. Our spirit spies detected unusual energy coming from a human in Tokyo. When I arrived, I saw him for myself. The moonlight illuminated the sky as his spiritual power radiated from his body. There was no doubt—he was a Veilkeeper.

Then came the routine we'd followed for years. He was abducted and taken into the Spirit World, where I was forced to place him in holding. We gave him time to process the news and then essentially threatened him. My father's rules, not mine. I find them inhumane.

We tell them they can either accept their fate or stay in the Spirit World—a gentler way of saying they accept or die. Many fall into disbelief, hitting themselves or crying, convinced they'll wake up from what they assume is a dream. Children agree more quickly. They think it's all a game—until they learn it isn't. I hate it when we have to bring children into this.

Kosei retired at sixty-seven when we discovered two more Veilkeepers on Earth. We sent out spies, and over a decade later, we found them. The first was eleven-year-old Jude, also in Japan like Kosei. He trained under Kosei and caught on quickly. The second was ten-year-old Maeve, living in America.

Years passed. Now, Maeve is nineteen, and Jude is

twenty. The two have never met. That was about to change.

Gwen, my assistant, entered my chambers as requested. She was always prompt, on time, and reliable. My sister Aurora once had an assistant too—one who was always late, always slacking off. My father set an example with both of them. Now, Gwen and I act fast. When my father says jump, we ask how high—and what's next?

"I'm here, sir," Gwen said, approaching my desk.

"Oh, good. Any word?"

"Yes, sir. I spoke to Jude as you asked," she reported.

"How did it go?"

"I can tell he's anxious, but he appears up for the challenge. He's heading to Kosei's compound to train now."

"Perfect. And Maeve?"

"Well, there was some trouble. I couldn't contact her. Her security team has changed since the last time I was in the States, and the number I called is no longer in service." She sighed.

"Again?" I grew annoyed.

That was the problem with dealing with a celebrity. Maeve became a famous pop star at fifteen, making it harder for us to reach her—or for her to handle assignments.

Fortunately for her, we never reported her defiance to my father. Her team usually handled her duties in her place. But this time was different. My father requested both Veilkeepers for this mission.

"Do you want me to reach out to her team? Maybe Marina?" Gwen suggested.

"Yes. Call Marina and tell her to get Maeve on the phone ASAP," I ordered. "This case requires both Veil-keepers. Orpheus and Dante won't be able to take this one."

Orpheus, a sorcerer, and Dante, a demon hunter, joined Maeve's team when she first awakened. They had been covering for her for years. I wished I could rely on them again. But my father gave strict orders, so I had no choice but to impose once again.

"I'll contact Marina," Gwen said, crossing her arms in thought.

"I'm sure she's still with Maeve. Those two are inseparable."

I prepared to make my trip to Earth. Jude would handle the mission fine—but Maeve? Convincing and tracking her down would be another matter.

No matter what she decided, we both knew she ultimately had no choice.

Chapter Two
Maeve

Marina pulled me aside before the video shoot.

"Gwen is trying to make contact," she said.

I knew that wasn't a good thing. This wasn't some friendly check-in or a casual "Hey, how have you been?" No, I knew exactly what it meant. It was time.

I had managed to avoid my duties for years. I had help, and I had been lucky. But this time was different. I had to face the music—no pun intended, though life was already unfair enough.

There I was, standing under the bright lights, sweating, my freshly done makeup already melting down my face, stinging my eyes. I couldn't even see who was watching me. The music started, my auto-tuned voice blaring through the speakers as I lip-synced and smiled, matching my gestures to the lyrics. I felt like a sideshow joke. I knew if I messed up, my mom and dad wouldn't let me hear the end of it.

They had promised me that after this music video, I could take a much-needed "break"—their way of saying,

Time to focus and start writing your next album, and it better be better and more chart-topping than the last. Their biggest fear was that I would become what they called a "washed-up has-been." Never mind that I had won seven Grammys and was only nineteen. It wasn't enough. Nothing was ever enough for my parents.

Through the blinding, unbearably hot lights, I could somehow see my mom trying to coach me from the sidelines. My dad stood next to some man, talking and shaking hands, likely making plans for my future without me.

"And CUT!" the director yelled.

I sighed in relief and took a deep breath as I walked over to my chair. Marina handed me a water bottle without a word.

Marina had been by my side through it all. I met her around the time when I was first summoned as a Veilkeeper. She wasn't human, but you wouldn't be able to tell—except for her eyes, that switched between a light red to a deep maroon depending on her mood, that might be a dead giveaway. People overlooked it, assuming it was just part of her beauty. She had shoulder-length turquoise hair, naturally that color, but everyone just assumed she dyed it.

I told my parents that if they wanted me to survive this music career, I needed Marina with me. She had been there since I was ten, and I was grateful she decided to stay. Only I knew what she really was. My parents were clueless, and that's how it needed to be.

I lived a double life: Veilkeeper and pop star, never

just Maeve Tyler. My stage name was "Daisy Maeve." I hated it. It was cringeworthy, but catchy.

My mom padded over to me. "That was good, but in the last scene, I want you to not look so lost in the final frame. Smile when you sing the word 'mine,' but don't smile too big."

Marina handed me a tissue to wipe my eyes, bringing some relief from the eyeliner irritation.

"All right, Mom."

"Good. Don't mess up. Your dad and I have places to be after this. Don't make us late by dragging this out any longer."

I gave her a sarcastic thumbs-up as she walked away. Not like I wanted to be there either.

Marina gave me a tight smile.

I couldn't wait to get out of here, to be free of this ridiculous, itchy costume. But I knew I wouldn't get to rest for long. If it wasn't my parents wanting something, it was Aurelius.

Any poor excuse for a "break" from my music career would come to a screeching halt the moment I found out what Gwen wanted to tell me.

Chapter Three
Jude

Kosei was old. He was pushing eighty, yet he was still in impeccable health. I could only hope I'd move like him when I reached his age.

I arrived at his compound the night before after talking with Gwen about my next big case.

Kosei's compound sat deep within a remote forest, surrounded by dense woods and breathtaking scenery. It was a sanctuary, perfect for training. The entrance was marked by a traditional Japanese torii gate, leading to a stone pathway winding through a meticulously kept garden filled with vibrant flowers and towering trees. The main house—a traditional Japanese-style building with sliding shoji doors and tatami mat flooring—exuded rustic simplicity and historical charm. It had everything: a spacious training hall, living quarters, a meditation room.

Adjacent to the main house was an expansive training ground equipped with wooden dummies, sparring rings, and designated areas for martial arts and spiritual exercises. A Zen Garden, with raked gravel, strategically placed stones, and a koi pond, offered a space for reflection. A natural hot spring on the premises provided a private retreat for relaxation and healing. The entire compound pulsed with spiritual energy, reflecting Kosei's immense power and dedication to refining his craft. This was a sacred place for warriors seeking mastery.

So far, though, when it came to Veilkeepers, I had been the only one training here. Others came and went, learning techniques, but none were forced to bear the burden of saving the world—except me and that girl from America.

I was lucky. I lived close enough to train under another Veilkeeper like Kosei. That gave me an advantage. Not to mention, being a guy, I had the upper hand over Maeve Tyler—the other keeper.

I never thought I'd meet her. She was some hot-shot celebrity, and she lived on the other side of the planet. No one from my team had gone to see her, either. Still, I had to admit—it would be interesting to talk to her and about her experiences.

My team was small. Just four fighters, including me. Kosei helped on occasion, but for the most part, it was us handling cases.

First, there was my best friend, Soren. We'd gone through grade school together, always picking fights—either with each other or with idiots who thought they could take us on.

Then there was Ryu. A Pyrofiend—a fire demon, if you're not familiar with the term. Pyrofiends weren't exactly known for being friendly, which is why I never took his bad attitude personally.

Ryu had a twin sister, Marina. An aquatic apparition —a sea demon. She lived in America with Maeve. In all the years I'd known Ryu, I'd only seen him speak to his sister once. Not surprising, considering Ryu barely talked at all. Sometimes I'd say something to him, and he'd just walk right past me. Used to annoy me, but now I just accepted it.

Despite his loner tendencies, Ryu had become one of the most loyal people I'd ever met. He always pulled through when we needed him most, and honestly, our team wouldn't have been the same without him.

Not that he had a choice. Before joining us, Ryu had racked up a criminal record. I remember when Aurelius gave him an ultimatum—aid a Veilkeeper or be locked up for a hundred years. I wasn't sure how long a century would feel for someone aging in demon years, but Ryu clearly didn't want to find out.

And lucky for us, he brought Caelum with him.

Caelum was an apparition with the ability to manipulate nature. He was also a warlock—one of the strongest I'd ever met. I wouldn't want to be on the receiving end of his power. Maybe that's why Ryu originally chose to fight beside him instead of against him.

With my team, I never saw the need for Maeve to join us or ever join forces with her team when it came to missions. They handled things on their end, and I held up my end of the bargain in this corner of the world. So when Auri told me she was coming along for this mission,

I was confused. I never needed her help before, why was this any different?

Something about this whole thing didn't add up.

Chapter Four
Marina

I met up with Gwen down in the lobby. I wasn't expecting her to get here so fast, but she arrived as soon as we wrapped up the shoot. All I could think was—wow, this case must be urgent.

She filled me in on the mission. I didn't know how to tell Maeve.

"Please don't make her go—" I said, knowing it was useless, but I had to try. Maeve had just finished filming the music video for the last single on her album. The pressure was already on her.

Usually, Jude or the other allies handled cases. Maeve hadn't fought in almost five years. Her powers had weakened over time, and she hadn't kept up with her training.

I remembered the first time I met her. She was around ten years old and had just found out she was a Veilkeeper. She, Orpheus, and her older brother Troy were working on a case. I was already familiar with the occupation because I had spent the previous year working with Jude and my brother, Ryu.

When I saw Maeve—this sweet, trembling little girl—I just knew I couldn't leave her side. Despite being destined for this life, I always felt she wasn't truly made for it.

Her brother Troy didn't possess any real power. He was just an eleven-year-old kid himself at the time, but he was good at giving Maeve an alibi from her overbearing parents.

Her parents had always treated their kids like two walking dollar signs. Since childhood, they'd been on TV and performing, their parents desperate for one of them to make it big. Once Maeve started writing her own songs, they worked day and night to put her on the map. Her father used what connections he had to land her a record deal. Her mother bleached Maeve's naturally black hair—with its unique dark lavender tint—to make her blonde.

And that was it. She gained unwanted attention. She was a superstar, a pop powerhouse. She couldn't go anywhere without fans lining up, screaming, flashing their cameras, and throwing things at her. The same went for the paparazzi. Sneaking away for missions became nearly impossible without her being recognized.

"No, this time Maeve has to go," Gwen sighed.

Odd.

We walked up to Maeve's hotel suite, passing through security. They nodded and let me through without a second glance. Gwen's eyes widened, taking in the whole setup.

I knew what she was thinking—if Maeve actually used her powers, she'd be far stronger than all of her security combined.

I knocked on her door. I knew I could just walk in, but since Gwen was with me, I wanted to make sure Maeve was decent.

"Maeve, it's me. Gwen's here."

There was no answer.

I opened my satchel, pulled out the keycard, and swiped it. No Maeve in the living room. I walked over to the bedroom and saw the bathroom door closed.

"Maeve?" I knocked.

I heard whimpering on the other side. I knew that sound. She was crying.

I walked back to the living room, where Gwen waited.

"She'll be out soon," I confirmed, gesturing for her to take a seat on the couch. I sat diagonally from her on the loveseat, curling my legs up onto the seat and leaning against the armrest.

Gwen nodded and sat down.

"It goes without saying—wherever this mission is, I'm going with her."

"Of course," Gwen agreed.

"Do you think my brother will be there?" I asked, genuinely curious.

Gwen shrugged, then tossed her pale pink ponytail behind her back. Her sparkling eyes glistened with uncertainty.

"So far, I think it's just Jude and Maeve."

"Oh wow, and they've never met. How does he

expect them to just work this case together? Just the two of them?"

Gwen looked uneasy, like there was more to this than she was letting on—or like she truly didn't know and was wondering the same thing.

"Where is it?"

She pulled out her phone and opened the maps.

Yes, even spiritual beings had cell phones, apparently.

She zoomed in on a remote coastal area, closer to Maeve than Jude.

"Oh, well, at least no one will recognize her there, I hope," I said. "Great. So what exactly is going on?"

"We're not sure. Apparently, strange demonic activity that the King of the Spirit World wants the Veilkeepers to investigate."

That didn't sound any different from any other case to me. Why couldn't the other team members check this out first? Why specifically Maeve and Jude? Did the king just want them to meet? Why run the risk of sending both Veilkeepers? Normally, they were kept separate in case something unfortunate happened.

This didn't sound like a case Jude couldn't handle with his team. Or Orpheus. Or Dante. No—something was up. And I had a feeling Gwen knew that too.

It was hard to trust Aurelius and Gwen because, despite seeming to care about Maeve, they had their own agendas, their own mission, their own loyalties to the Spirit World.

I had to be the one to look out for Maeve.

I wasn't a strong fighter like my twin brother. He was

the complete opposite of me. He was a destroyer; I was a healer. He was fire; I was water.

But knowing Maeve hadn't fought in years, I would have to help her with this. Even if it meant changing everything I was. I loved her too much to let her do this alone.

Maeve finally emerged from the bathroom, wiping her eyes. She smiled at Gwen and took a seat next to me.

"Oh good, you're here," Gwen said with a warm smile.

Maeve returned the kindness. "I heard everything," she said in a soft, low voice. "So it'll just be investigating and maybe a few demons?"

Gwen gave her a sad look but still smiled weakly. "As far as Aurelius and I know right now."

Maeve looked at me, and I looked back. I placed my hand on her leg—partly to comfort her, and partly to stop it from bouncing up and down. She did that a lot when she was nervous.

"Okay."

Maeve took a deep breath, tucking her long, warm-toned golden-blonde hair behind her ears. Her eyes were still wet, her nose stuffy, her cheeks blotchy from crying and scrubbing off her makeup.

"I can do this. I'll be ready."

Gwen glanced at me.

"You know, I bet Jude will bring Soren—especially once they find out you're going to be there."

Soren?

Oh, goodness gracious. Poor Soren. He was something else.

Maeve let out a small laugh. She had never met Soren, but she had heard plenty of stories.

I met Soren years ago when I worked with Jude and my brother Ryu. Soren was Jude's childhood best friend. He was known as the class clown, always getting into fights with kids from other school districts. He and Jude stayed in trouble for brawling.

So when Jude became a Veilkeeper, the role suited him—and of course, Soren didn't shy away from helping him.

Soren used to be crazy about Gwen when he was younger, but eventually, his attention turned to me.

Every time I saw him, he'd grab my hands and confess his undying love for me. It was cringey but kind of sweet—if you were into that sort of thing.

I was older than him. He was twelve and I was sixteen when I first worked with their team in Japan. Now he was twenty-one and still sending me emails, texts, and letters every chance he got.

I hadn't seen him in person for a while—Maeve's schedule kept me busy—but it would be interesting to see Soren again.

He was a funny guy, and maybe he'd help lighten the mood.

Because aside from demons and mysteries, I had to wonder—considering Jude's cocky, abrasive personality—how well he and Maeve were actually going to get along.

Chapter Five
Soren

Jude called me and told me about the mission. I was looking forward to going with him—just in case he needed a helping hand. I knew the other guys wouldn't be too thrilled about traveling so far to some rundown, sketchy town on a part of the map I'd never even heard of.

The thing is, though... he didn't exactly invite me to go with him. Yet.

I was headed to meet Jude, who had just gotten back from training at Kosei's. He was at his girlfriend Kayo's house.

Once inside, I spotted Jude sitting across the table. He nodded at me. Her parents and all her cute friends were there.

"Hi, Soren! Hee hee," they all giggled.

"Hello, ladies," I greeted, striking a pose and closing my eyes. I knew I was a good-looking guy. Who could blame them? I was tall, muscular, and had luscious light brown locks tied back to perfect my mysterious, hip look.

Yeah, I was a cool guy. Nobody could argue that.

However, despite my undeniable charm, there was only one girl in the world for me—my beautiful merlady, Marina.

My heart had belonged to her since I first laid eyes on her. Every time I saw Maeve on TV or a billboard—since she was some big-shot worldwide superstar—I thought of Marina standing nearby, always by her side. Maeve was so lucky.

Marina seemed so far out of reach, almost impossible to get in touch with. I sent letters, emails, and texts. She was either too busy to reply or gave very short responses.

But when I heard about this mission, all I could think was—this is my chance. My chance to finally see her again.

She was beyond beautiful. No girl in my hometown, college, or even in this room could ever compare.

Even though Jude hadn't exactly agreed to let me tag along on this case, it was summer break. University had just let out. I had every reason to go.

Besides, he'd never admit it, but he needed me there. He didn't know what the hell he was walking into.

Jude always liked to act tough. His girlfriend was the only one who could really put him in his place.

Those two had been together since elementary school.

He was just like me in that way—once you knew you'd found the one, you knew. Nobody was ever going to come between Kayo and Jude.

We sat, talked, and ate.

Finally, Kayo's parents went upstairs to bed, and all her cute friends left.

"Bye, Soren," they all said in unison.

"Later, ladies," I grinned.

As they walked away, Jude walked up next to me and sighed.

"You look like such an idiot."

Kayo laughed.

"What? They dig me!" I defended.

"Do they, though?" Jude said.

Boy, was he in a bad mood. I knew why—he had to explain to Kayo that he was leaving soon for another mission.

I thought about it, and maybe now wasn't the best time to ask if I could join. Tensions were already running high.

Kayo was smiling so big at him as he sat down next to her on the couch, arms crossed, eyes closed, about to break the bad news.

I sat in the chair on the other side, reclining with my feet kicked up, ready to watch the showdown.

"What's wrong?" she asked him.

Kayo was beautiful. She had long, straight dark brown hair that went down her back and honey-brown eyes.

She usually wore her hair half-down, tied in a bow at the back. She was the good girl—always making smart decisions and getting straight A's, while my dumbass best friend Jude stayed in and out of trouble.

Not that I could talk much.

Jude finally spoke.

"Auri and Gwen called. The reason I was at Kosei's all weekend is because I was called to do another mission."

That happy grin Kayo had vanished.

"Oh," she said.

The room went silent.

I clenched my ass cheeks together, trying so hard not to fart and break the silence in the worst possible way.

I knew it was going to be a loud one. I could feel it brewing.

"When?" Kayo asked, her head hanging low in sadness—or maybe disappointment.

"Friday. This week," Jude told her.

I started racking my brain, trying to figure out my schedule. I'd need to find someone to feed my cats while I was gone.

I kept waiting for those two to hurry up and finish talking so I could chime in with, *Don't worry, ole buddy, ole pal, I'll be right there with you.*

My stomach churned loudly. They both looked over at me.

"Are you okay?" Jude snapped.

I gave a thumbs-up and a grin that said, *don't mind me.*

"So, how long will you be gone?" Kayo inquired further.

"That, I don't know. It's off the edge somewhere near the States, a remote coastal town," he answered.

"Is it just you and Soren, or will Caelum and what's his name... Ryu be there?"

"Well, apparently, it'll be me and—"

"Me too!" I shot in quickly, jumping a little in my seat, my ass erupting loudly at the same time.

They both cut their eyes at me.

"Uh, excuse me," I muttered, turning blood red.

"So just you and Soren, huh? It must be a short mission," Kayo said, perking up a little.

"Well, no, not exactly—ha, haha." Jude was so nervous.

Kayo narrowed her eyes.

"What are you not telling me, Judei?"

This was painful to watch, and my stomach was hurting again.

I knew I had to get to the bathroom soon, or I'd be done for, but I couldn't stand up without the risk of my ass exploding mid-air.

I had to sit there and wait, trying to suck it back up as I watched my boy fight for his life.

"So, do you remember me telling you about how there's another Veilkeeper in America?"

"Yeah, the singer Daisy Maeve," Kayo answered. "What about her?"

"Well, you know how we've never met, right?" Jude kept laughing nervously.

I was shifting and rotating my ass cheeks, trying not to let another one escape.

The more I held it in, the bigger it felt like it was getting.

This motherfucker was going to be loud if I didn't release it soon.

But I couldn't do that to my boy—he would never

bring me around again, and I'd definitely lose my chance to go on the mission.

Then I could kiss my dream of seeing Marina goodbye.

"She was also summoned. Maeve—she's also going on the mission," Jude said, bracing himself.

Tough guy—until it came to Kayo.

"Oh, so just you and her, huh?" Kayo looked away.

"Well, no, Gwen texted me. She said Marina will be there too."

"Oh, got it. So just you and two very pretty girls alone together on some coastal retreat getaway?"

"No! It's not like that. It's for business."

"Sounds like business and pleasure."

God, I hope so, I thought, still clenching tightly.

"Kayo, baby, it's not like that."

"Then I'm coming too!" she demanded.

"What? No way. It's way too dangerous!"

Kayo rolled her eyes and looked away, a tear forming.

She wasn't usually the jealous type, but I got it. If your man was running off to a secluded beach with one of the biggest pop stars in the world, that would cause concern.

I would be there, though—to make sure my boy didn't slip up, and of course, to have a romantic rendezvous with my long-lost love.

Kayo turned to me.

"Soren, you'll be there, right?"

I nodded.

"What? No! I didn't agree to that!" Jude shouted.

I couldn't argue with him. My ass cheeks were clenched to their max.

I just sat there, smiling through the pain, tears welling up in my eyes.

"You just want to go because Marina is going to be there!" Jude accused.

I couldn't even respond. I couldn't breathe without farting.

"Oh, great! So it'll be a double date! Cool!" Kayo got up and stormed off.

"Kayo, no! Wait!" Jude chased after her.

I waited until I heard the back door slam... and finally relaxed, releasing a thunderous fart.

I sighed in relief—then turned around and saw Kayo's dad standing behind me, holding a glass of water, just staring at me expressionless.

Chapter Six
Aurelius

It was clear that everyone knew something was up—Maeve and Jude especially. Why else would they both be summoned for what seemed like such an easy mission, compared to the ones they'd faced before? Gwen filled me in on how hard Maeve took being called for the task. Between this and her parents constantly breathing fire down her neck, the poor girl never got a chance to do what *she* wanted.

I wondered what kind of excuse Marina would even come up with to get Maeve away from her parents. Whatever it was, it had to be a good one—there was no way of knowing how long this mission would take.

I hadn't forgotten about Jude either. He had plans to spend summer with his girlfriend Kayo, and I shot those plans straight to hell.

It's a wonder these kids didn't all hate me.

I had no choice.

But I do, from time to time, feel guilty.

If I had the powers myself, I would've just become a Veilkeeper.

It was that sort of thinking that got my sister in trouble.

I had to stay stern in my stance. This is business. It isn't personal.

No—this is fate.

It can't be helped.

Oh, but the price they've all paid—Kosei, Jude, Maeve—the things their destinies have taken from them...

Of course their safety was a concern of mine, but I could never guarantee it.

I arrived in the town of Starbrook.

It was a small coastal town with a population of "everyone knows everybody and everybody's business."

It might be hard to work here.

Everyone might be in awe or overly curious about the strange new people staying at the local Hummingbird Inn.

And not to mention Maeve being recognized. If the media got wind of her being here, we were done for. The streets would be lined up.

Luckily, the people here seemed cut off from the world—old-school in the way they didn't spend all day on the internet.

In most homes, it looked like they still had a single house phone—not handheld access to the rest of the world.

I scoped the town out. I didn't sense anything right away, but something felt off. There was an eerie feeling.

I saw the local inn where we'd all be staying. It was an old, maybe five-story building with moss growing up the sides and chipped paint.

I walked inside to find older furniture, and the floor creaked with every step.

It definitely wasn't a five-star hotel, but it would have to do.

"Hello!"

An older gentleman in fisherman attire greeted me. "Welcome."

"Nice day to you, sir," I tried to act human.

He smiled.

"I'd like to book four rooms."

"Four?" His eyes went wide, clearly shocked by the request. "What, do you have a whole party coming to town? Family?"

I knew this would happen. People were going to be curious—that's how deserted and forgotten this place was.

He'd probably tell everyone he knows—which is everyone—that some strange, tall man in weird robes (my only clothes) came in and booked four rooms in an inn that probably sees four guests a year.

Of course, that's an exaggeration, but honestly, I wasn't sure how the place was still running.

"Four rooms it is!" he said. "Does it matter which floor?"

"Not at all."

"Well, we're short on help. Two will be on the second

floor, one on the third, and one on the top—if that's okay. That'll give you the biggest rooms we have if we split it up like that."

"Sure, sounds great."

I couldn't care less. Jude would probably arrive first anyway, so he'd get first pick.

As the man prepared the keys, I glanced outside. I saw a lot of elderly people.

A lot of them looked happy enough—nothing strange right off the bat.

My father, King Aurelius, had been vague during the briefing. Which meant there was only so much I could tell the team.

He'd said: *Strange demonic energy coming from Starbrook. I will need to summon both Veilkeepers for this mission. No exceptions. No substitutions.*

Naturally, Gwen and I both had questions. But we did what we were told.

We summoned them.

Now we wait.

We were just as clueless as they were.

"Here you go," I received the keys.

"If you need anything, just let me know. People here are friendly, so don't be afraid to ask for help with directions.

Not that there's much town to get lost in," he chuckled.

"I appreciate your help. Thank you."

"Ah, it's nothing! Feel free to ask for anything at all during your stay. I'm always here except for at night. Oh, and one more thing..." He leaned slightly forward. "Try to avoid going to the beach at night if you can."

That caught my attention. I didn't want to look defiant or ungrateful, so I responded with a polite, "Oh?"

"Yeah... good-looking guy like yourself? She might get ya!"

I tried not to narrow my eyes.

Who?

Get me how?

"Yeah, just be careful. Take care of yourself."

I wanted to ask more, but just then the phone rang.

He turned to answer it promptly.

"Inn," he said as his greeting. "Oh, hiya Bill! What's cookin'?"

I didn't want to seem weird by just standing there watching him talk on the phone, so I turned to walk away.

He nodded at me as I did, still talking to Bill.

I stepped outside. The air was humid and sticky.

There was a gloom hanging over the afternoon from the thick clouds.

It would be a while before the team arrived.

I decided I'd return to the Spirit World until then.

I just couldn't accept what my father told me—which was basically nothing.

I needed more answers, especially if I was sending my people into this. I didn't want them going in blind.

If I were to speak with my father, I'd need to appear detached. Unlike Aurora, I'd need to let my curiosity come across as tactical—me wanting to know where to start with the mission.

Not in a way that made it seem like I had any genuine concern for the kids.

"Pardon me," said a kind old couple walking arm-in-arm, as the woman accidentally brushed up against my arm.

The people here were kind.

I didn't want whatever was going on to get worse and cause them any harm.

I walked behind a building, out of sight from the townsfolk. I closed my eyes tightly—and vanished.

Evaporated into thin air.

A technique both Gwen and I possess.

I would return to the Spirit World to confront my father.

I only hoped this time, I'd leave his unsettling presence with more information—and fewer questions—about what to expect.

Chapter Seven
Jude

I called my good friend Caelum on the phone. He was one of the teammates I briefly mentioned earlier. I trusted him more than anyone—he's never let me down. The guy possessed incredible power, and I figured I'd need him for this mission.

Soren wanted to go and had been begging me nonstop. I still hadn't given him a clear answer, but he wasn't gonna stop bugging me until I did.

"Hello?" Caelum answered. "Jude?"

"Hey, what's up, man," I said. "How you been?"

"Fine, really. And you?"

I could tell he was curious. I wasn't much of a *phone* guy.

"Nothing much. About to start a new mission."

"Oh yeah, I know. Soren already filled me in," Caelum replied.

Of course he did, I thought.

"Well, listen—I don't want to keep you long. Are you interested in joining me?" I asked.

There was a short silence.

"Well, uh, actually... I would, Jude. But things with my mom aren't too good right now," he said solemnly.

"Oh. I'm sorry to hear that, man." I meant it.

"Yeah. But you should take Soren. By the way it sounds, you shouldn't have too much trouble. And listen —if things get bad and you do need my help, I'll be there."

I'd forgotten about Caelum's situation with his mom. Caelum is a demon spirit that was reincarnated here on Earth. He spends his days in his human form but has the ability to awaken his demon powers.

His mother raised him alone. Same as my mom. That was one of the things he and I had in common.

Him and his mother were really close—until he got a little older and started noticing changes. She became more forgetful, more distant. Eventually, she spent most of her days in bed. The doctors diagnosed her with a type of depression.

Caelum had been taking care of her ever since.

Despite initially using her as a vessel to take form again, he grew to love her.

He didn't have a father—because, well, the type of transfer he did to get here didn't require or involve the usual process of reproduction.

Her husband at the time—back when she was pregnant with Caelum—grew suspicious.

Why did his wife give birth to a red-haired, gray-eyed baby when both of them had jet-black hair and dark brown eyes?

His mother blamed it on recessive genes, but her husband couldn't cope.

He assumed she'd cheated and left her. She raised Caelum alone ever since—until she got sick.

Now he takes care of her.

I hated asking him for help with this case. I really did.

But I also really didn't want to take gooey-eyed, love-struck doofus Soren.

I thought about asking Ryu, but that guy lives off the grid. Doesn't have a cell phone and keeps his demon energy muted.

Caelum's usually the only one who's good at finding him.

"No, it's cool, man," I told him. "Take care of your mom. I'll reach out if we run into trouble and need extra help."

"Thank you and good luck," Caelum said before we hung up.

I sighed and fell back into my desk chair in my room.

Then I heard a noise downstairs—sounded like someone had just come through the front door. It was either my mom, Soren, or Kayo.

They were the only ones with a spare key to my house. Kayo lived about three houses down. Soren lived a street over.

The three of us grew up together. My mom even considered them family.

I heard someone aggressively coming up the stairs. I recognized the footsteps—and sure enough, my door swung open.

It was Soren.

"PLEASE LET ME GO, MY GUY!" he begged. He was not letting up anytime soon.

I sighed and threw my head back, spinning in my desk chair.

"Fine..." I muttered.

"Wait—no way. Really?" he asked, shocked I'd caved.

"Yes. You can come. But you better not embarrass me."

He grinned so hard and squinted his eyes so tight I thought he'd get stuck that way.

"Oh no, not me!" he said. "You've got nothing to worry about!"

I slapped my hand to my face and leaned back again.

I couldn't wait for all this to be over—and it hadn't even started.

Soren started doing some stupid little victory dance around my room while I completely tuned him out.

He was saying something about Marina again.

I drifted into thought and found myself thinking about my own girlfriend.

She still wasn't really talking to me.

All her texts had been short and passive. I could tell she was still mad.

She didn't like the idea of me being alone with the other Veilkeeper.

But what she didn't realize is that she had *nothing* to worry about.

I had zero interest in getting to know this "look at me" attention-crazed pop star.

Honestly, I found her music cheesy and annoying. It was so bubblegum it made me cringe just to hear it.

Kayo didn't believe me, but I knew how I felt.

I'd get this done, survive being stuck with these people for however long, save the town, and come home to be with her again—and *only* her.

I loved her.

And if it were up to me, I'd never have to leave her side.

Soren was still doing that stupid dance.

I really hoped something came from his almost decade-long crush on Marina.

I prayed her feelings would be reciprocated—or maybe she'd just tell him to give it up already.

It was kind of sad at this point. I felt bad for the guy.

"I'm going home to pack!" he shouted, leaping out of my bedroom like he damn near floated down the stairs.

I guess I should pack too.

I pulled out an old duffel bag and just slammed some clothes in, along with a spare toothbrush.

I wondered how many bags a high-maintenance celebrity like Maeve was gonna bring to this thing.

I zipped up my bag and tossed it on the floor.

I checked my phone.

Kayo still hadn't responded.

I'd tried to go see her earlier that morning, but her dad said she wasn't home.

I'm not entirely sure that was true, but I didn't push it. I didn't want to aggravate her further. I'm not Soren.

I laid on my bed, arms behind my head, staring up at the ceiling.

I'd be ready for whatever enemy was coming.

I didn't mind going into battle.

But I wondered how long it had been since the other Veilkeeper had actually fought or used her powers.

I had a feeling I'd be the one pulling all the weight—and not because she's a girl.

No—I'm not some sexist piece of shit.

But because it always seemed like she had other people fighting her battles for her.

Yeah, I worked with my team on missions.

But I didn't just send them out and stay behind.

That shit sounded lazy. Weak.

Like she was avoiding what she was called to do.

As far as I was concerned, Maeve was an insult to what a Veilkeeper even was.

I had more respect for Dante or Orpheus—the other fighters on her team.

They never backed down.

I wished it was one of them I was meeting for this mission.

I closed my eyes and drifted off.

I needed to rest while I could.

Because there was no telling what this case might bring.

And I had a pretty strong feeling... I'd be dealing with it alone.

Chapter Eight
Maeve

I told my parents I planned to go off somewhere with Marina for an undisclosed amount of time to focus on writing my next album.

They told me I had six months—and that they expected a full record written and recorded with Jace, my producer, by the time they heard from me again.

No "good luck," no "I love you."

No "try your best."

Just you better have it done.

I wasn't surprised. That behavior from them was pretty standard.

Regardless of where I was really going, it was good to get away from them.

I grew up precocious and always did what I was told. I never talked back or questioned anything.

I just smiled and performed like I was supposed to.

The only problem now was that I was running out of things to write about.

Most of my songs were about love and friendship.

But the love I wrote about was the kind I saw in movies... or what I witnessed between Orpheus and his wife, Cleo.

I've never actually been in love.

Sure, I've had boyfriends—but that was a long time ago.

So now here I am, fresh slate.

I needed inspiration.

But that would have to wait. Hopefully this mission wouldn't take too long.

Marina walked into the hotel room with her computer.

We were still staying in the suite Gwen had visited us in during our time in New York.

"Let's video chat with Orpheus," Marina encouraged, like that would somehow cheer me up.

I had wanted to ask him if he'd join us, but it sounded like Aurelius made it very clear: only the Veilkeepers were to go.

And despite what people believed... as scared as I was about these missions, I hated having to ask Orpheus and Dante for help every time.

Dante and Orpheus used to be rivals, but my work as a Veilkeeper brought the two of them together.

Now—whether they admit it or not—they're close friends.

Sure, they clashed and bumped heads constantly in the past, but they always pulled through and worked as a team.

We defeated so many evil demons because of them.

I wouldn't even be alive without their help.

Marina sat on the couch with her laptop and placed it on the coffee table in front of me.

I took a deep breath. "Have you told him?"

"Yeah, we texted," she confirmed. "He wanted to check in with you before we go."

I played with the ends of my hair.

They were starting to look so damaged from all the bleaching and toning to maintain this blonde color.

My natural hair was very dark, so getting it to this warm-toned blonde had been exhausting—and honestly, I was tired of it.

Marina looked at my hair. "Should we change it for the mission?"

I raised my eyebrows.

Like my hair could handle another dye job.

It definitely needed a cut, though.

But my mother would kill me.

Even though I'm technically an adult, anything I do with my appearance has to "fit the brand."

Marina read my mind—or at least it felt like she did.

"Never mind."

"Yeah," I agreed. She knew how my parents were.

I typed the password into the laptop and pulled up the video chat app.

I clicked on Orpheus's name and waited as it rang.

It started to connect... and then there he was.

Orpheus was older than us—maybe mid to late thirties.

He's tall, skinny but muscular, with short, wild brown hair that he usually kept out of his eyes with a headband or a bandanna.

He hadn't changed much over the years—except it looked like he was starting to grow some facial hair.

I hadn't seen him in a while.

"Ah!" he exclaimed when we all successfully appeared on each other's screens. "There she is!"

I smiled. "Hi, Orpheus."

"Maeve."

I felt myself tearing up just a little. It was so good to see him.

I wondered if he could tell I was scared.

"Cleo and her sisters have been playing your album nonstop," he said.

His wife, Cleo, was a triplet.

She had two sisters, Este and Leslie.

Leslie used to work closely with us back in my younger Veilkeeper days, while Cleo and Este were still away studying.

All three of them were witches.

Leslie taught me the little bit I know about spells and magic.

I was grateful for them.

"Tell them I miss them," I said, and I meant it.

We had a good run working together.

Before I became famous, I used to see them every day.

Now the four of them—along with my producer Jace —live on the coast of Rhode Island in a huge house.

I guess you could say that was our headquarters.

I miss being there with them.

"I will. So tell me, how are you feeling about this mission? Marina somewhat filled me in," he asked.

Marina glanced at me and nodded—that part was true.

"Well... I'm as ready as I'll ever be."

There was a pause.

He knew I was lying.

But he decided to go with a soft, "That's the spirit."

I gave a tight smile.

"Listen," he said. "If you run into any trouble—if you need help—don't be afraid to ask me. I'll be there. Just like before."

Those tears I was holding back started welling up again.

"I mean it, Maeve. I'll track down that rowdy shit-show Dante, and we'll come straight there."

"That means a lot," I told him.

"Nothing's changed. We may be living separate lives now, and I know our time gets eaten up with everything going on... but we're still a team. No matter how far apart we are or how long it's been.

I've got your back. So does Cleo, Este, Leslie—all of us.

Oh, and even Jace—who, by the way, said not to worry about the new album."

My heart skipped a beat.

How did Jace already know I was supposed to be writing?

I hadn't even called him yet.

My parents work fast.

Jace was also a demon—a water demon, just like Marina, but from a different clan.

He joined our team around the same time she did, back when I was ten.

He's also a DJ and loves music. He grew up in the human world.

Long story there. But he and I have created so much art together. He hypes me up in the studio, and I wouldn't want to work with anyone else.

Even though my parents keep trying to make me.

They're afraid our work is getting "repetitive" or "stale."

Their words.

"Jace?" I asked.

"Yeah. He said he'll brainstorm and work on a few things while you're on the mission. Said not to stress."

I exhaled, finally feeling a bit of relief.

I loved my team.

I could always count on them.

I needed to reach out to them more often. They were my chosen family.

They've never stopped supporting me. They've really gotten me through a lot.

And knowing that—even if they weren't coming with me—they still had my back going into this... it helped. A lot.

Which, I realized, was Marina's plan all along.

She wanted me to call Orpheus so I'd remember—I'm not alone.

I do have people in my corner.

People ready to come help if I need them.

"I love you, Orpheus. Thank you."

"I love you too, kid," he said. "We'll talk soon."

Marina waved and ended the call.

We looked at each other.

"Feel better?" she asked.

I shrugged. "Yeah... somewhat."

She sat with me a while longer.

I needed to start packing soon.

I didn't want to look extra, so I didn't want to take a lot of bags.

I wasn't even sure how to dress. Workout clothes, maybe? Leggings?

"Marina," I asked, "can you help me pack? I don't want to take too many bags."

"Oh yeah, of course."

I went into my room.

All my clothes were too bougie—thanks to my parents.

They didn't like when the media blasted pictures of me looking rough across the internet or slapped me on the cover of a magazine.

Then the rumors would start swirling.

Like once, I walked outside to grab something from the car—barely awake—and there was a paparazzo hiding in the bushes.

Got some shots of me and sold them.

Next thing I knew, my parents were calling me livid about the headline:

"Top News: Daisy Maeve Parties Hard— Morning After Walk of Shame!"

So yeah, even if I was just going outside for a few minutes, I had to be dolled up.

I hoped no one in the town of Starbrook would recognize me.

Maybe a hat and no makeup would help.

We'd see.

Marina and I pulled out two large luggage bags.

"We'll need to buy you some regular clothes," she said, flipping through my closet.

She was right.

I got online and looked up what we could get delivered in the next day or two.

Time was running out.

It was almost time to go.

I needed to be ready by Friday—in every possible way.

Chapter Nine
Soren

This place felt almost deserted.

Even the suburb I live in right outside the city back home was bustling and crowded compared to this.

The town was old, worn down—and the people looked the same way.

Jude had been calling Kayo nonstop.

She didn't want to see him off before we left.

She finally answered the phone.

They talked, and he agreed to call her every night to let her know what was going on.

She texted *me*, of course.

I showed my boy Jude.

The text said something along the lines of: *You better make sure Jude keeps himself in check, or I'll be equally mad at you if anything happens.*

I had never seen Kayo like this.

So possessive.

Maybe insecure?

But Jude had never put her in the position to act like this before.

This was new, uncharted territory.

Jude didn't have any girls that were friends—not even Kayo's friends.

He always has been, and still is, all about only her.

I tried to ignore their lovers' quarrel.

I only had one thing on my mind—and it wasn't fighting demons.

It was Marina.

We got off the bus, each holding the same duffle bags we'd had since junior high and arrived at the Humming-bird inn.

It looked old and crappy—like everything else around here.

Some might call it *rustic or full of character*, though.

Gwen was outside waving at us.

She was in a good mood, as usual, looking all shiny and perfect.

Her, in a town like this? She stuck out like a sore thumb.

Her pink hair and beauty would definitely have all the people here staring.

Gosh, just wait until they see Marina.

"Hey, boys!" she greeted enthusiastically, like we just showed up for a vacation.

I looked around, a little disappointed.

I didn't see Marina anywhere.

Gwen must've picked up on that, because the next words out of her mouth were:

"The girls are on the way. Sir Aurelius is bringing them."

Sir Aurelius.

I mean, yeah, I get it—he's a big deal.

But Jude and I always just called him Auri.

He never had a problem with it.

He wasn't one of those people who got offended over dumb stuff like someone being nice or trying to break the ice.

But Gwen was talking about her boss, so I figured that's why she said his name all formal.

"Let me show you boys to your room. You don't mind sharing, right?" she asked, holding open the door to the inn.

Yeah, I *minded.*

If it were up to me, I'd have my own room—just in case my love Marina wanted to come spend the night with me.

Oh well.

We walked in and saw a quaint, humble little lobby— old-looking, of course.

Old TV.

Old furniture from way back in the day.

Some of it was dusty.

I bet the rooms weren't any better.

We walked over to a—you guessed it—rickety-ass old elevator.

Honestly, I was surprised the place even had one.

I reluctantly got on with them.

Jude was quiet.

I guess he was just taking everything in, trying to sense anything unusual.

I was hyperaware of the supernatural, even though I'm not a *superhuman* like Jude.

I didn't sense anything major. Just your usual everyday stuff.

There's always something hanging around, it seems.

This place felt no different right off the bat.

Jude stood with his head down, eyes closed, arms crossed, as we rode up to the third floor.

The elevator doors opened, and the hallway looked so creepy.

The carpet was flat and old with some weird ugly pattern.

The floor creaked like I was going to fall through it.

"Here's your room. Oh—and the keycard," Gwen said, handing Jude the card.

"They only gave us one per room."

"That's fine," Jude replied.

"Okay, well, I'll see you guys once the girls arrive. We're having a meeting on the fifth floor in Sir Aurelius's room. He's got the big suite, so we'll all fit in there and talk. I'll text you when to come—Room 504."

Of course he does, I thought.

He's the boss. It made sense.

Not that his room's probably any better.

This whole building's one big piece of crap.

In my town, this place would've been condemned.

Gwen waved and walked off, her ponytail bouncing effortlessly as she turned to leave us.

Our room had two queen beds and a nice view of the ocean.

The door to the balcony was cracked open, and the room felt just as humid and sticky as it did outside.

There was a cool breeze out there, but when I sat on the bed, it felt damp.

I wondered if they'd just washed the covers and didn't give them time to dry—maybe they left the balcony door open to help?

Or maybe it was just all the moisture in the air.

Whatever it was, it was *annoying*.

Cold, damp.

I hoped it would feel better before we had to sleep in it.

Jude walked outside and leaned on the balcony, taking in the ocean view.

He still wasn't saying anything, so I decided not to bug him.

I unpacked my toothbrush and toothpaste, tried to find my breath mints.

I needed to freshen up before my true love arrived.

I couldn't stop thinking about how much longer it would be.

A part of me was also a little nervous about meeting Daisy—or Maeve—or whatever.

I'd never listened to her music; it was too girly.

But I'd heard it plenty in the background at the arcade and the grocery store.

I'd never met a celebrity in my life, but I figured if Marina liked her, then she had to be cool.

I looked out and saw Jude taking a picture of the ocean and texting.

He was probably letting Kayo know he made it safely.

I turned on the bathroom light—it flickered and buzzed before finally staying on.

I started to freshen up.

I took down my super cool man bun and redid it for that sleek, well-put-together look. Gotta look good for the ladies.

Jude's hair looked wild—like he hadn't slept in days, even though he slept most of the way here.

He didn't give a shit what he looked like in front of them.

I rinsed my face and grabbed a towel to dry off.

As soon as it hit my face, I caught the worst smell.

I pulled the towel off the rack, flipped it over... and there it was.

Some big, nasty brown "doo-doo" stain.

I dropped it instantly.

It looked like someone had wiped their whole ass with it, and the hotel just *tried* to wash it but didn't get it fully out.

I was shaking.

That was disgusting.

That was *demonic*.

Who does that?

And how long had it been there? That thing looked older than me.

I stood there in silence and left the towel on the floor.

I wasn't about to pick that thing up again.

And who was I even gonna complain to?

The little friendly old man I caught a glimpse of at the front desk?

This trip had already gone sideways.

All I could think was—it *better* be worth it.

Marina could never find out about this.

She'd *never* kiss me again if she knew I basically rubbed my whole clean face up against someone's ancient ass-crust.

I kicked the towel under the sink and ran water over my face again, even added some bar soap.

Let my face air dry as I walked out of the bathroom.

Jude was sitting on the bed, holding his phone on his lap.

"What's wrong with you?" he asked.

I must've still looked disturbed.

"Oh, uh... you don't wanna know," I told him.

"Alright," he said, not giving one single shit more.

I looked around the room in the natural light.

I *really* hoped the bed didn't have brown stains too.

Jude's phone buzzed.

He checked it instantly.

His eyebrow raised, and he started clicking away to respond.

"What is it?" I asked.

His face said it all—like there was more he wasn't saying—but I figured it was just his girl.

"Gwen just texted me," he said.

"They're here."

Chapter Ten
Marina

Maeve had been pulling on her hair ever since we left New York.

She does that when she's nervous.

Right at the top, near her hairline—she just tugs.

If you look closely, it's thinner than the rest. One day she's going to bald there if she doesn't stop.

I'm constantly swatting her hand away or distracting her to remind her not to do it.

I wasn't sure what was bothering her more—the mission or meeting the others.

I tried to give her a heads-up on what to expect, personality-wise, based on what I remembered.

I told her Jude could be arrogant, but not to take it personally.

He's strong, but just like her, he's relied on others for help too.

And Soren? Soren's a giant teddy bear.

I think she and he will get along well. He's funny,

and Maeve tends to laugh at everything—even when she's overwhelmed by things she can't control.

I told her it'll be okay.

That we'll all be there, working as a team, and we'd figure out what's going on in Starbrook *together*.

I kept emphasizing that she's not alone. Orpheus and the others are just one call away, too.

We arrived at the inn with Aurelius.

Maeve and I went into our room to put our luggage away.

The inn was in pretty bad shape, but Maeve was fascinated by it.

"It definitely has character—and has probably seen a lot," she said, looking on the bright side.

Despite being rich and living a luxurious lifestyle, Maeve's actually pretty down-to-earth.

The house she grew up in as a child was small. Both her grandmothers would take turns watching her during the summer, and she'd go back and forth between their homes. One house—only a few hundred square feet—sat at the top of a hill in a rough part of town.

If you stood in her grandmother's bedroom and looked out the window, you could see the Smoky Mountains in the distance.

Her grandmother had two large seashells she'd found when she was younger.

Maeve remembers going into her room, staring out at the mountains, placing a shell to her ear, and listening to what her grandmother said was *mermaids singing*.

That memory is permanently engraved in her, and it brings her peace whenever she thinks of it.

Maybe, being near the ocean, we could find a shell.

And if Maeve started having anxiety, she could imagine she was safe back at her grandmother's house, listening to the mermaids.

I was clearly desperate. But I needed something—anything—to calm her down.

Because when Maeve has anxiety, she doesn't just worry.

She has *full-blown* panic attacks.

Her body goes into fight or flight.

Sometimes she swings.

Sometimes she hits herself.

Sometimes she bolts out the door—and I've found her hyperventilating, convinced she's about to die.

She feels like something is *off*.

Like death is near.

Like she's being hunted and no one can stop it.

We've gotten better at managing it, spacing out the episodes.

But I'm still afraid for her.

Being here, in a strange place, with unfamiliar people and an unknown enemy?

Even one of those things is enough to spiral someone out of control.

I blame it on her constant drive to be perfect.

She never wanted to make a mistake—because if she did, her parents would punish her for it.

"Maeve," I said as we finally got ourselves together and headed upstairs to meet with Aurelius and the others.

"Yeah?" she turned to me.

I could tell she had her brave face on.

"It's going to be fine."

She exhaled and raised her eyebrows.

"You ready?"

She gave me a thumbs up.

I laughed. I knew there was a little sarcasm in that gesture.

We walked into the hallway and shut the hotel room door behind us.

Maeve led the way, still trying to show me she wasn't scared.

She pressed the elevator button hard—like she had to make sure it registered. It was loose and old.

We stepped inside.

Another deep breath came from her.

"I think he said Room 504, right?"

"I think so," I agreed.

The fifth-floor light blinked.

The elevator beeped.

The doors shakily opened.

We walked a little way down the hall to Aurelius's suite.

"Here we are," she said.

And froze.

All I could think was: *please hold it together.*

Now is *not* the time for a panic attack.

She'd done so well so far. She hadn't fallen apart yet.

I knew she couldn't control it—but I hated seeing her like that.

Out of control.

Feeling like it was the end.

I knocked on the door when I noticed she was still frozen.

"Thank you," she whispered to me.

I gave her a "I got you—don't worry about it" smile.

Gwen opened the door. "Hi, girls," she said, stepping aside to let us in.

I led the way this time. Maeve followed behind.

The room was similar to the suite we'd had in New York—except older and smaller.

But it still had the sitting area separated from the bedroom.

We walked over to the two couches facing each other.

Aurelius was standing between them, ready to start the meeting.

On the couch to his left sat Jude.

Just as I remembered him—except taller.

Short, messy black hair with a dark bluish tint.

Arms folded. Staring straight ahead like he was either annoyed or deep in thought.

And next to him?

Soren.

Good ole Soren.

Grinning, smiling at us like a goofball, waving and showing all his teeth.

I couldn't help but smile back. He looked so ridiculous.

I turned to see Maeve's reaction—she was smirking, holding in a laugh.

"Ladies, have a seat," Aurelius said, gesturing to the opposite couch.

The tension in the room was thick.

I sat across from Soren.

Maeve sat across from Jude.

"Well, might as well get introductions out of the way," Aurelius said.

"Guys, you already know Marina. Soren, Jude—this is Maeve Tyler. Maeve, this is Judei Yamamoto and Soren... uh..."

Aurelius blanked.

Soren looked mildly offended. "*Tsurugi*," he said. "I'm Soren Tsurugi."

"Right..." Aurelius muttered.

The room fell quiet.

Soren was staring at me—hard.

I could feel it.

But my eyes were locked on Maeve and Jude.

Maeve sat up straight, unsure of what to do.

Jude didn't smile at her.

He just sat there, relaxed but sizing her up.

I didn't know if he was trying to sense her power—or trying to intimidate her.

Maeve sat stiff, like she was being tested.

Like she wasn't one of the biggest pop stars in the world.

It had been a long time since I'd seen her look *this* intimidated.

Usually, people are that way when they meet *her*.

Until they realize she's as down-to-earth as they come.

"It's nice to meet you, Judei," she finally said.

"It's *Jude*," he retorted, snappy.

"Yeah," Soren laughed. "He hates being called his full name."

He laughed again, awkwardly, trying to lighten the mood.

"Oh—Jude. Sorry," Maeve corrected herself.

Jude just sat there, staring at her.

Finally, he looked away—to Aurelius—signaling he was ready to begin.

Aurelius spoke.

"All right. We're all here today because there have been reports from Spirit World officials of unusual demon activity in the area—which we all know."

Gwen walked up behind me and took a seat on the arm of the couch.

"I don't have a radar map yet to show where the energy is coming from," Aurelius said, "but I will shortly. Gwen?"

"Yes, sir," Gwen piped up. "It's on its way."

"Thank you. Now—according to the reports, some of the villagers have been attacked.

They didn't survive.

They made it to Spirit World and asked what happened... and all they remembered was seeing a black shadow before dying."

"Well, that sucks," Jude muttered. "How many were killed?"

"Around six so far."

"Six?" Soren said. "Isn't that, like... half the town's population?"

He laughed awkwardly. It failed.

Nobody said anything.

Even Jude flinched and looked more annoyed.

"Once the radar map gets here, we can maybe pinpoint where the demons are coming from."

"Are we sure it's demons?" Maeve asked.

Jude looked over at her.

"I mean—I know they're not human, but..."

"What *else* could they be?" Jude snapped. "He said they sensed demon energy."

"I know," Maeve said quietly, looking down at her hands. "But maybe... could they be ghosts or aliens from outer space?"

"That's a good point, Maeve," Soren chimed in, trying to support her.

We all looked to Aurelius.

"Unfortunately, we're not entirely sure," he said. "But it *is* leaning more toward demons."

"So how are they here? And why are they randomly in this place?" Maeve asked.

"That's exactly where this gets interesting," Aurelius said, holding up one finger.

"We believe someone—or something—opened a portal to the Demon World here. Or some other dimension. But again, it's leaning toward demons, because that's the energy that was detected."

"A portal? How?" Jude asked.

Maeve looked uneasy.

"That's what we're trying to figure out. The passage to and from the Demon World is a *controlled* journey—Spirit World has full authority over it.

If someone managed to open their *own* entrance...

let's just say they'll never see the outside of a Spirit World cell again."

"Oh—you mean that cell you locked *me* in when I was ten and told me I had to start risking my life doing things like this?" Maeve said suddenly.

The room went *dead* quiet.

Jude adjusted his posture, sitting forward.

"So I find the guy or woman who opened the portal, we seal it, and we go home. Sounds easy."

"You say that like you've done it before," Aurelius replied.

"Well, once the map gets here and shows us where the energy is, it'll be obvious what I need to do."

I noticed how Jude kept saying "*I.*"

Like Maeve wasn't even here.

"Slow down, cowboy," Gwen jumped in. "We're not even sure *how* to seal the portal if it was created with apparition energy."

"What?" Jude looked at Aurelius.

"It's true. We're still working out the logistics," Aurelius admitted.

Jude leaned back, rubbing his eyes, elbow on the armrest.

"Don't get discouraged," Gwen added.

"We've got people in Spirit World working around the clock. Researching. Figuring this out."

"You mean to tell me that, as long as demons have been around, no one thought to plan for this?"

"I don't think you understand," Aurelius said, voice rising.

"Creating a portal to another world is no small feat. Some *gods* can't even do it.

This has *never* happened before. And yes, we've explored the 'just in case' scenarios.

But we came up empty.

Now we're scrambling to solve it before more than six people die."

Maeve's hands tightened in her lap.

They were wrapped together—white-knuckled.

I knew she was thinking what I was thinking:

This mission isn't going to be as quick or simple as we were led to believe.

Aurelius had discovered new information. That much was obvious.

Not only were we facing an unknown enemy—

Six people were already dead.

And a portal to the Demon World might be open *somewhere* in this town.

Demons were running rampant—not the nice, civilized kind.

These were monsters.

And whoever created that portal?

They were probably nearby.

Closer than we knew.

We were going in blind.

And all I could think was:

Why does Aurelius think Jude and Maeve alone are enough to handle something this big?

He's still not telling us everything

Chapter Eleven
Maeve

On the way back to our room, Marina and I didn't speak. We rode the elevator down with Jude and Soren. While Soren seemed nice enough, Jude was very standoffish and acted cold toward me.

"Should've taken the stairs. It's only two floors," he bitched when we were on the slow elevator. I don't know—maybe it just seemed slower because I was on there with him.

Soren kept smiling at us. I thought his face might be permanently stuck that way. Marina kept giving him side-eye glances and the occasional polite smile.

"So, uh... would you ladies want to grab dinner?" Soren offered.

Before I could decline, Marina spoke up. "Oh, that's okay, Soren. Maybe another time. Maeve and I still need to get settled. But thank you."

"Oh." He looked crushed.

I saw Jude try not to laugh, but he still somewhat snickered.

"Yeah... another time," Soren said, disappointed.

Their stop came. The elevator doors usually opened slowly, but this time they did it aggressively.

Jude hopped out without saying a word. Soren walked behind him, still looking at Marina. "See you soon," he said.

Once the doors closed and we started moving again, we rode in silence.

I couldn't tell what Marina was thinking, but all I could think about was contacting Orpheus and Dante ASAP. There was no way I was going to handle this mission without them. I physically couldn't. This sounded bigger than anything we've ever faced before.

"You know, I am kind of hungry. Are you?" Marina asked, breaking the silence as the elevator doors swung open to the second floor.

"Yeah, but I don't want to eat with them," I responded.

"No, I know. I meant let's get something—just you and me," she said.

That sounded great. I was starving.

We kept riding the elevator down to the first floor. The doors were back to opening slow, which was crazy— it was like they could sense Jude's negative energy.

We walked through the lobby and saw the same guy sitting at the front desk, watching a small TV hanging high up on the wall. It was box-shaped, one of those older models from way back when. My grandmother used to have one in her kitchen. For a second, it reminded me of her—but a long time ago. That TV isn't there anymore at her house, and but then again neither am I.

The guy nodded at us, then went back to watching his show. It looked boring, but he could barely look away.

We exited the hotel and stepped outside.

"There," Marina said, pointing to a small, low-key restaurant.

"Sure," I agreed.

We walked across the street and a couple buildings over to the quaint little restaurant. It had small wooden tables and chairs, and one other person eating alone.

"Hey!" greeted a friendly woman who looked to be in her early to mid-fifties. I was nervous. I hoped she wouldn't recognize me. I'd just remembered I forgot my hat at the hotel.

"You girls sit anywhere—I'll be right with you," she said.

We took a seat at a table in the corner. The menus were already on it.

I sighed. I was exhausted. I didn't even want to think about the meeting or what we'd talked about—but I knew it was about to be up for discussion.

Marina, who was usually good at reading my mind, brought it up instantly.

"Well, that was a lot," she said.

I nodded. "Sure was."

The woman came over and took our drink orders. We browsed the menu, and suddenly I didn't feel hungry—even though my body was weak from it. Funny how your mind can play tricks on you. But the thought of demon portals and dead people didn't help my nerves.

"I wonder what the townspeople here think about the

random disappearances and people just found unalive," I asked.

Marina raised her eyebrows. "Yeah, I know. And not to be morbid, but I wonder what condition the bodies are found in."

"Oh gosh."

"Yeah, I mean, some demons just feed off your soul and suck it right out of you without leaving a scratch. And others will rip you to shreds. So I wonder how these people are being—"

"Yeah, that's okay. I got it."

"Sorry," she said.

"No, it's not you," I apologized. "I'm just not sure I'm going to be able to survive this."

"What?" Marina asked. "That's crazy. Of course you will." She grabbed my hand. "You know we always find a way out of messed up situations."

I pulled my hand away. She was right. It's true—we usually did find a way through. But this time... I'm not so sure.

"We'll call Orpheus as soon as we get back to the room," she suggested.

"Can it wait till tomorrow?" I knew it wasn't a smart idea, but I was so exhausted. I really didn't want to have to put on a brave face for him while also asking for help.

Marina was hesitant at first, but then she answered, "Sure. Of course."

The woman came back with our drinks and placed two glasses of water in front of us. I wondered how clean it was, since this place looked just as run-down as the hotel we were staying at. Marina and I both ordered the special since neither of us took the time to read through the menu.

We sat there for a while, not saying much of anything.

Until it dawned on me.

"Marina," I said.

She looked up, her big red eyes meeting mine.

"You were in the Demon World before—and you came here through a portal?"

She nodded. "Yeah, I did. My brother and I spent the first few years of our life there with our mom."

"Didn't you say your brother was a fire demon?" I whispered.

"That's right."

"Well... since you guys are twins, wouldn't that make you part fire demon too?" Not sure how I never thought to ask this until now.

Marina giggled a little. "Not exactly, Maeve. Demon DNA is tricky and works differently. My mother was an aquatic demon and my father was fire. While I do possess some of his DNA, his powers and abilities were only passed on to my brother, Ryu. I took completely after my mother. I may have my father's eyes and a few facial features... it's strange, huh?"

"Yeah, I don't get it," I confessed. "I mean, I do—but I don't. If that makes sense."

"Think of it like this: say two humans have a baby. The mother is a pianist and the father isn't. The baby is still human, just like both of the parents. But the baby also happens to be good at piano, like the mom. So, while I'm a demon, my abilities and talent are in manipulating water. My brother's gift is fire, like our dad."

I sat there and processed that for a bit. "Oh..."

"Understand now?"

I nodded.

She smiled and went back to staring into space.

I did too—until I remembered the main part of my question, which I'd gotten distracted from.

"But you came here through a portal?"

"Well... yes. I did. But not by choice. I was actually kidnapped by humans and demons that were in alliance with each other."

"I vaguely remember something about that when I was younger."

"Yeah. I told you before, when we first met," she said.

I sat up, ready to hear the story again, and she—as usual—read my mind.

"At the time, there was someone in the Spirit World working with a group of demons and humans running an illegal operation. I just so happened to fall victim to it. I was kidnapped in the Demon World and brought here to the Human one. I was held captive until my brother tracked me down and saved me. Then I stayed here. I worked with Jude and my brother for a while... before I met you. And I've been here ever since."

The mention of Jude made my stomach twist again. He was such a dick.

"Was Jude always such a dick?" I slipped and said out loud. Marina probably already knew I felt that way.

"No. The Jude I knew back then was actually really

nice," Marina said. "I'm not sure what was up with all that attitude and tough guy act today."

"Yeah, me neither. It was so uncalled for."

Marina nodded. "For real."

"So, wait—one more thing. You said someone in the Spirit World was involved in that weird operation. What were they planning on doing to you when they kidnapped you? And... if someone from the Spirit World was in on it, does that mean you came through the main portal—the one that's supposed to be the only way to and from the Demon World?"

The woman came back and set down our food. It looked like roast beef with carrots. I wasn't entirely sure. We thanked her and waited until she walked away before continuing.

"The portal was the main one, yes—because there's only supposed to be one. And they were planning on selling me."

"Selling you? Like... into slavery?"

Marina nodded. "Some kind of slavery, yes."

I didn't want to talk about it anymore. The thought of someone being that cruel to Marina made my blood boil. As long as I've known her, Marina's never hurt a fly. To me, she wasn't like other demons. I trusted her. She never showed signs of being violent. She was good.

I picked up my fork and started stabbing the meat on my plate. Marina did the same. It didn't look like we'd be getting much to eat tonight. Not just because the food looked questionable—but because so did our time here.

Chapter Twelve
Jude

I sat on my bed and opened a bag of chips. They were all crushed from being in my duffle bag, but I still needed to eat. Soren had tried to go to dinner with Marina and "Useless," but they declined. I probably wouldn't have gone anyway—although I was starving.

"Hey, man," Soren said, walking up way too close to my bed. "Give me one of those chips."

I looked at him like he lost his mind. "No way. Get your own," I said, stuffing a handful of broken chip pieces into my mouth.

"Come on, man. I haven't eaten since we left home."

I stopped chewing, my mouth still full, chip crumbs flying as I spoke. "That's your problem. Leave me alone. These are my chips."

Soren's whole vibe shifted. He stiffened and got all serious. "Listen, Jude. I've shared food with you plenty of times when your mom was too drunk to cook dinner. Now give me a damn chip!"

That pissed me off. He brought up my mom? Really?

"Fuck you," I said. "Now I'm really not giving you any. And that was your parents who invited me to dinner. Not you."

He balled his fists at his sides like he was about to start something. "Yeah, because I asked them to invite my sorry-ass, poor excuse for a friend over."

"What did you say to me?"

"You heard me, you selfish turd face."

"I'm not the one that wiped my face with a shit towel!"

That did it. He stepped forward and pushed me while I was still sitting down.

"You said if I told you about that, you wouldn't say anything!" he yelled.

I stood up, got right in his face, and shoved him hard —hard enough to knock him backward onto his bed.

"What's your damn problem, Jude!?"

"You are! Now let me eat my fucking potato chips!"

He looked like a bull seeing red. I picked up another chip, held it to my mouth slowly, and smiled just to rub it in that I still had the bag—probably expired, knowing my mom, but still mine.

"Mm... so good," I said dramatically.

Soren launched off his bed like a tank, ramming into me full force and tackling me to the floor. The bag of chips went flying. Bits of crushed chips exploded all over the place.

"Soren, what the fuck!" I shouted after getting my breath back. "My potato chips!"

"Fuck you and them old crusty chips!" he yelled as we wrestled on the floor.

I regained control, slammed him down, and pinned him into the carpet and the mess of chips. He kept trying to get up, but even though I was skinnier, I was stronger. Veilkeeper perks.

He kept twisting, trying to flip me, but I slammed him back into the crumbs again, scattering them across the room.

"You ain't shit, Jude!" he yelled.

"You ain't shit!" I yelled back. Real creative.

He fought harder, nearly getting me off him, but I kept control.

"That's why Marina don't want your weak ass," I shouted.

"That's why Kayo won't return your calls!" he fired back. "Because you're a selfish jerk!"

I laughed in my head. Yeah, I'm such a selfish jerk—risking my life to save the world from a demon apocalypse. Sure.

"Get off me, Jude!"

"Not until you chill out!"

"You're heavy! Probably from hogging all the damn chips!"

"The chips you made me spill everywhere!"

"Good! That's what you get, stupid head!"

Right when I was about to respond, we heard a loud knock on the hotel door.

"Boys, are you in there?" a familiar voice called out—muffled but clearly Gwen.

We froze, both of us still lying in the middle of the room surrounded by crumbs. Too cool to admit we got startled.

"Boys?" she said again.

We scrambled up. I tried to help Soren off the floor, but he swatted my hand away.

We walked to the door like nothing happened, casually opening it. Aurelius and Gwen stood there, both staring at us like they were trying to figure out what disaster they were about to walk into. Auri raised one eyebrow.

"Is everything alright?" he asked.

"Yeah," we both lied.

Honestly? It kind of was. We'd been fighting like that for as long as I could remember. Just how we were.

Soren still had chip crumbs in his hair and all down his back.

Auri and Gwen stepped inside. Their eyes scanned the disaster. Towels tossed in the bathroom. Chips everywhere.

Auri sighed and rolled his eyes. "You guys just checked in today. Is it really going to be like this? Is there even going to be a room left when it's time to leave?"

"What?" I said, pretending to be clueless.

"The room. You guys already destroyed it," Auri said, starting his lecture.

"It was his fault!" Soren snapped.

"You started it, you damn idiot!" I fired back.

"You're a damn idiot!"

"No, you're a bigger idiot!"

"You're a—" he started before Gwen interrupted.

"Boys, enough!" she snapped. "Sir Aurelius is in your presence. Act like you have some kind of sense!"

Sir Aurelius. Like I was supposed to bow or something. Yeah, okay.

"Thank you, Gwen," Auri said, turning to me. "Jude, I think we need to talk."

"Right, finally, you've come to your senses!" I said, crossing my arms with confidence, smiling with my eyes closed like I already knew what he was going to say.

"What do you mean?" he asked, eyebrow lifting again.

"You know!" I said. "This mission is too big now and you want to bring out the big guns. Send 'Useless hope I don't break a nail' delicate daisy home."

Auri grimaced. "Well... yes and no."

"Huh?" I opened my eyes. "What part of that was a no?"

"I'm not sending Maeve home. She's a part of this."

"And a Veilkeeper just like you," Gwen added.

"It's time you started acknowledging that," Auri continued.

I rolled my eyes. "Yeah, sure. Whatever."

"As far as bringing in the 'big guns'—your words, not mine—I do think we're going to need more help than we originally expected."

"No shit," I slipped out. Gwen gave me a look that could kill. I smiled nervously. "I mean—you're the boss. I agree."

Auri paused for a second, then continued. "Gwen and I contacted members of your team. Ryu and Caelum are on their way now."

"Alright! Now that's what I'm talking about!" I said, punching my fist into my hand.

"Oh great," Soren muttered, rolling his eyes. "Ryu..."

Yeah, those two didn't get along. Probably because Ryu thought Soren was an idiot—which was ironic, since Soren wanted to marry his twin sister. Dumb.

"They should be here in the next day or so," Auri said.

"How'd you find Ryu so fast?" I asked. "It's not like the guy has a phone or an address."

"Or anything normal" Soren added, thinking back to the time we really needed Ryu but had no clue where he was. He's a great teammate—when we can find him.

"Caelum had already located him and gave him a heads-up. He was on standby," Auri explained.

"Ah. Makes sense," I said. "Now this is more like it. Those weak ass demons don't stand a chance!"

Auri shut his eyes briefly, then opened them again. "I hope you're right, Jude. Tomorrow, the plan is to start questioning people in town while we wait for the others to arrive. Even if the radar map comes through tonight, we'll most likely hold off until Ryu and Caelum get here. Still, talking to the townspeople about what they've seen —or lost—could give us a lead."

"Why do we care what they were doing?" I asked.

"Isn't it obvious, numb nuts?" Soren jumped in. "He's saying one of them might've opened the demon portal. Duh."

"A human?" I asked.

"We don't know who lives here. We've never had issues in this region before, but that's why it's important to learn this town's history. Who's new? Who doesn't belong?" Auri said. "You saw how they acted when we arrived. If someone new showed up recently, they'd remember."

"Got it," I said. All I could think was—we had a lot of work to do. This might not be such a short mission after all, like I told Kayo.

If she'd answer her phone, I'd fill her in. I sent her a picture of the ocean earlier and all she texted back was, "Enjoy." But I knew better, I could sense the sarcasm from here on the other side of the world.

She's not going to be thrilled when she finds out we're staying longer. Maybe she'll ease up once she hears the guys are coming. Maybe then she'll stop calling this case a double date.

Auri and Gwen left not long after, telling us to be up early and ready.

I tried calling Kayo one last time before bed. She texted back: "busy."

Yep. Still mad.

She was going to make me chase her. I knew it. I'd have to go back groveling, swearing she's the only one for me. I couldn't imagine losing her—especially not over Useless Maeve.

I turned off the light. Soren had cleaned the chip crumbs off his back and collapsed onto his bed too.

I lay there with my eyes closed, trying to sleep, but my mind was all over the place. I was pretending I didn't care, pretending I was tough. But the truth?

Someone here was powerful enough to open a demon portal from the inside.

And that's who I was supposed to face.

What if I wasn't strong enough?
What if I never saw Kayo again?

Chapter Thirteen
Maeve

Gwen sent Marina a text saying that Auri had decided to bring two members of Jude's team here to Starbrook—one of them being her brother.

As much as meeting her brother sounded appealing to me, I was still disappointed they didn't decide to ask Orpheus or anyone else I'd worked with before. I was kind of over meeting new people —especially after how poorly meeting Jude had gone.

One might think that since we were both Veilkeepers and had both been through a lot, we'd have loads to talk about. It's not like there are many of us—just me, him, and the older guy, Kosei, who I still haven't met. But after Jude, I wasn't sure I wanted to meet him either. Those two train together.

It never occurred to me what they thought of me. I'd never gone to see them—not because I didn't want to, but because I never had the chance. My parents always kept me on a tight leash.

What if Jude thought I was some kind of snob? On top of thinking I was weak?

It's not true that I'm weak. But am I as strong as Jude? Heck no.

I haven't trained or fought in years. Every time I used to harness my energy, it would even surprise me. But on the spot, I couldn't always summon it. That part was on me. I didn't have time to figure out my abilities the way Jude did. Mine show up sporadically and at random.

It's no surprise he sees me as an anchor more than an asset.

I laid in bed, unable to sleep. Marina was already conked out. I was going to ask her how she felt about seeing her brother again after all this time. Apparently, he doesn't even own a phone, so she has no way of contacting him. And from what I gather, he hasn't made much effort to reach out to her, which I find... odd.

Soren always writes to her. Email, texts, calls—even love letters sent to the house in Rhode Island where Orpheus and the others live. He always finds a way to remind her she's on his mind.

Ryu, her brother, does not.

It's not like he doesn't care. Surely, he does—he went out of his way to save her when she was taken from the Apparition World.

Still... it's odd.

I walked over to the window. It was pitch black out there—no lights along the beach. I thought maybe some fresh air would help ease the anxiety. Maybe a short walk would tire me out.

I decided to sneak out of the room without waking

Marina. I pulled on a sweater over my gray T-shirt and pants, carried my slides to avoid heavy footsteps, and carefully slipped into the hallway. I double-checked to make sure I had the key card in my pocket, then shut the door gently behind me.

Once I was outside the room, I slid my feet into my shoes and shuffled down the hall to the stairwell. I wanted to exit from the side of the building, not the main lobby—just in case the front desk guy wanted to make small talk.

It wasn't a big deal. We were only on the second floor.

I opened the stairwell door. The lights inside flickered and buzzed loudly.

At the bottom, I came to two doors—one led out to the beach, the other to the lobby. I picked the one that led outside.

The wind hit me hard. It was blowing aggressively —not exactly cold, but definitely not summer-like either.

I made my way closer to the shore, hoping the wind wouldn't blow sand into my eyes.

The waves were crashing violently. I couldn't tell how big they were until they slammed into the shore, then rolled back out.

I sat right in front of the massive, dark body of water.

There were some lights further down the beach to my right—probably from nearby businesses—but they were dim.

I sighed and took in the quiet.

Then I started wondering—if a demon showed up

right now, would I be able to fight it? Would I be killed right here on this dark, abandoned beach?

I could see the headline now: *Pop Star Daisy Maeve, Dead at 19.*

The article would read: *Found dead on Bumfuck Beach. Still investigating.*

I thought about how my death might affect the people in my life. Marina would be devastated. She never hid how much she loved me—and I felt the same. I knew she'd take it hard.

My parents? They'd be mad they lost their cash cow, but probably make a fortune off the spike in music streams after I died. I'm pretty sure all my money would go to them. Not like a huge chunk of it doesn't already, the way my contract is set up.

They always blow through their share. They tell me I wouldn't be this successful if it wasn't for their "connections" and them "riding my ass" to work harder. And once they blow through the money, they ask me for whatever I've saved—or they start guilt-tripping me into booking more interviews or shows.

So no, they wouldn't care because I'm their daughter. They'd care because I was their retirement plan.

Jude would laugh. He'd probably say "I told you she was weak" to everyone.

I considered going back inside. I wasn't about to give any of them the satisfaction of something killing me.

Just as I stood up, I froze.

Down the beach, a figure was walking—slowly, not directly toward me, but in my direction.

Closer to the water. Feet getting wet.

It looked like a woman. Slender. Long black hair. A white nightgown.

I squinted, trying to see better.

She had a bit of a limp. And a strange glow—maybe just the way the nightgown caught the light.

As she got closer, I noticed the gown looked dirty. Old.

I brushed sand off my pants and backed away slowly. That walk turned into a jog. Then a run.

The creepiest part was that her long black hair looked like it was completely covering her face. I told myself it was just the wind blowing her hair, but she wasn't trying move it out of her face so she could see. She didn't seem normal.

When I reached the inn's side door, it was stuck. I had a mini heart attack thinking I was locked out.

Then it yanked open. I slipped inside. The wind slammed it shut behind me.

I peeked through the glass window into the lobby and saw Gwen and Auri sitting on the couches.

I stepped in. They both looked startled—like I'd walked in on something they didn't want me hearing.

"Maeve," Gwen said, eyes wide.

"What are you doing up?" Auri asked, sounding like a dad.

I smiled. "I'm a grown-up now, Auri. You didn't say we had a bedtime."

Gwen smiled at that and looked over at him.

I glanced around and noticed no one was at the front desk. The lights behind it were off. Most hotels had someone on the night shift, but not at this one.

Auri sighed. "How long have you been creeping around?"

"You mean, did I hear what you were talking about? No. But I did go out to the beach—and I saw something kind of weird," I told them.

"You went out to the beach?" Gwen asked, looking at the sand still on my pants and shoes.

"Yeah. Just for a while."

"Do you find that wise, Maeve?" Auri said in that lecture-y tone.

"Well... no, not really, but—"

"Maeve, you need to stay close," he cut in. "We don't know what to expect or what we're dealing with here."

"Promise you won't go out again?" Gwen asked sweetly, like I was still a child.

They were starting to sound like parents.

"Fine."

Gwen smiled, but Auri still looked annoyed. He was even grouchier than usual tonight.

"I'm heading back up," I told them.

"Wait," Gwen said. "You said you saw something weird. What did you see?"

They both looked at me. Auri crossed his arms, waiting to hear.

"I saw a woman in what looked like old clothes—an old, dirty nightgown. She was staggering. Her hair covered her face. Something about her seemed... off."

"Did you sense anything? Like what kind of energy she had?" Gwen asked.

"Was she human, Maeve?" Auri added.

"No... I mean, I couldn't sense anything. I haven't been able to, not for a while," I admitted, looking down.

It was true. I hadn't had that ability in some time. Jude would've sensed her easily, I was sure of it.

Gwen looked sympathetic. Auri's expression didn't change.

"You can go to bed now," he said.

"Auri and I will go check it out," Gwen added, giving me a wink.

I smiled, grateful they at least believed me.

"She went that way," I pointed from inside the lobby, realizing that wasn't much help. "Down the beach."

"Goodnight, Maeve," Auri said.

Gwen waved.

I waved back and jogged toward the stairs.

Back in the second-floor hallway, I checked my pocket—making sure I hadn't dropped the key card on my little night outing. Still there.

I was tired now. Finally.

It hit me just before bed—when I walked in on Gwen and Auri, they definitely looked like they were talking about something they didn't want me hearing.

I told myself I was being paranoid. Maybe they were secret lovers or something, sneaking in a late-night chat.

I climbed into bed without waking Marina.

After a few moments of anxiety about what tomorrow would bring, I gave in to the exhaustion I'd been fighting all night.

Tomorrow would come, no matter what. Torturing myself with worry wouldn't change it.

All I could do was hope—whatever it is, I'd be ready.

Chapter Fourteen
Soren

The sound of waves crashing against the shore woke me up. I felt sticky and hot again. Then I noticed Jude had the balcony door open—he was outside, talking to someone on the phone. I figured it had to be either his mom... or Kayo, if she was finally speaking to him again.

I sat up and wiped the sweat from my face. I couldn't use a towel because of last time, but I still needed to look my best—I was going to be around Marina today.

Jude came back in. He looked like he was in a much better mood than yesterday.

"Oh good, you're up," he said with a grin. "I won't have to kick your lazy ass out of bed after all."

"Yeah yeah, shut up," I said jokingly. "I'm older than you. I needed more sleep."

"Dude, what? You're older by less than a year. Six months maybe."

"Shut up," I said again, heading to the bathroom. I wasn't sure what time we were supposed to meet the others, but I didn't want to be the reason we were late.

I got dressed, and about twenty minutes later, we were leaving the room. I glanced up and down the hallway first.

"What's your problem now?" Jude asked.

I laughed. "Just making sure no one sees us."

"Sees what?" He raised an eyebrow.

"You know… two guys leaving a hotel room together. People might get the wrong idea about me."

Jude sighed and kept walking toward the elevator.

"Not that there's anything wrong with that," I added. "The two fellas and a room thing. Just not for me. Because I'm not into that sort of—uh—"

"You're just digging yourself deeper," Jude cut in. "There's never anyone else here anyway. And even if there were, I doubt anyone gives a shit. Get with the times, man."

"Oh no, I'm with the times. I'm so with the times. Just not gonna get down with you. Or any man."

We got on the elevator. As the doors closed, Jude gave me a look—a mix of concern and annoyance.

"Are you trying to tell me something, or are you just babbling because you're nervous?"

"Nervous? Why would I be nervous?"

"Gee, I don't know—green-haired girl probably waiting downstairs, aggravated that you took forever to get up."

"Hey, you could've woken me. But no—you were too busy on the phone!"

"What am I, your mom? Your alarm clock?" he said, stuffing his hands in his pockets and looking away like he was in a music video. Jude thinks he's so cool. Whatever.

"Who were you on the phone with anyway?"

"Kayo."

"Oh, I knew it. So she's talking to you again, huh?"

"Yeah, I guess," he replied. "I sent her a text saying, 'Well, if you don't hear from me again, I'm probably dead.'"

"What?! You did not."

"I swear."

"Why the hell would you say something like that?"

The elevator dinged, finally reaching the lobby.

"You heard Auri yesterday. Shit's about to get real, and I don't know what to expect."

"Oh, what happened to 'Mr. Confident I'll be done in a few days—I don't even need your useless help, Soren'?"

"That last part still holds up."

"Shut up," I muttered.

We passed the same guy at the front desk. He raised his coffee mug and nodded.

"Boys. There's fresh coffee in the pot," he said, gesturing toward what looked like a relic from ancient times.

I glanced at the rusted, crusty coffee pot. It looked like it hadn't been cleaned since before I was even conceived.

"Uh... no thank you," I said, waving as we walked out.

Outside, we saw the others. The girls were already there, dressed in workout shorts and T-shirts. Marina looked especially beautiful today.

"Hey," I greeted, smiling before I could stop myself.

"Hi there," she replied. "How are you guys?"

"Ready!" Jude cut in. Back to his confident self, I guess. This man just told his future wife he was probably going to die... and now he's Mr. Cool again.

Aurelius stepped forward, and we all turned toward him.

"The radar map is ready," he said. "But Gwen and I need to return to the Spirit World to retrieve it and speak with my father. He's summoned us."

"I thought someone was bringing it?" Maeve asked.

"They were. That was the original plan. But my father asked them to hold off since he needs to speak with me anyway," Auri explained.

Maeve looked nervous. Like a "please don't leave me" kind of nervous. I felt bad. Even though Auri isn't really a fighter, he was one of the few people she knew here. Jude being a jerk wasn't helping.

"You'll be okay," Gwen said kindly.

"Tch." Jude crossed his arms like he didn't need the reassurance. He was making me cringe.

"Today," Gwen continued, "we want you guys to gather as much information as you can around town. Talk to the locals. Find out what they know about the deaths and disappearances."

"You may have to pull it out of them," Auri added. "A lot of them don't want people knowing something like this is happening here. They'll try to protect Starbrook's reputation."

I was listening, but I was also praying he told us to split up—because if so, I was definitely going with Marina.

"I think you guys should split up—"

"YES!" I shouted before Gwen could even finish.

She narrowed her eyes at me. Maeve chuckled a little, which was nice. She didn't seem so bad. I didn't know what Jude's problem was.

"Veilkeepers—check out the outskirts," Auri said. "Together. Work together in case you run into trouble. Avoid the woods until we bring back the radar."

Jude rolled his eyes.

"Okay," Maeve said softly.

Which meant—

"Soren, you and Marina stick together. Go into town. Try to talk to people. See what you can find out," Auri said.

I tried to act cool.

"Right," Marina said.

"We'll try to be back by dusk," Auri added. "Be careful. Don't do anything reckless. I don't want to see one of you walking into the Spirit World as we're walking out."

I didn't get it at first—then realized he meant don't get killed.

They turned to leave. Marina hugged Maeve, then walked toward me with the most breathtaking smile aimed right at yours truly.

"Shall we go?" she asked.

"Well... see you two later!" I called out, maybe too enthusiastically.

Jude gave a half-hearted wave. Maeve smiled with her eyes closed.

"Best of luck," she said.

Marina and I walked off together. This was what I'd been waiting for—an entire day with her. I'd forgotten how short she was next to me. When we first met, we were the same height. Now, I towered over her like a promising young, sharp, handsome man.

"So—" I said. "Where do you think we should start?"

Right then, my stomach let out the loudest, most monstrous growl of all time. Like, the whole world went silent just so it could roast me harder.

She giggled. "Well, I'd say... maybe somewhere with food?"

I laughed, rubbing the back of my neck. "Yeah, haha... sounds good. Sure."

Stupid body. Always betraying me.

We walked down the street. I told her all about the towel incident and the potato chip catastrophe from yesterday. She smiled and listened.

We reached a place right along the shore that looked like it served food and drinks.

"They should be selling lunch by now," Marina said, checking her watch. "It's a little past eleven."

"Yeah, this place looks fine."

We walked in. It was dimly lit, mostly from the windows. A few people were already drinking. I didn't judge. I just wanted a cheeseburger.

Marina walked up to the bar. The guy smiled at her, then glanced at me. He placed two coasters down.

"May I see your food menu, please?" Marina asked in the sweetest voice.

"Sure thing," the man replied, handing her a menu from behind the counter.

He looked way older than us. Like... old. And his face

—not his weight, but his face—reminded me of a hog. I wasn't trying to be mean. Just being honest.

"Thank you," she said, flipping through the menu. "Look—they have cheeseburgers. Isn't that your favorite?"

My face lit up. She remembered.

"Why yes, it is," I said.

"You should get it."

"Don't you want anything?"

She shook her head. "Maeve and I ate earlier. Protein bars and shakes. They worked."

"Well, if you change your mind, let me know."

"You're sweet."

My face went red. I hoped she didn't notice.

The bartender came back. "You folks new in town?"

"Yes, just visiting," Marina said.

"What for? Beach?"

"Yeah," I lied.

"Well, be careful—especially at night. You want to order?"

"Oh—yes," Marina said. "One cheeseburger. No pickles."

No pickles. She remembered that, too.

"You got it," the man said, heading to the back.

I noticed he was missing a leg. He had a peg. Like, a literal wooden peg. And just like that, I felt terrible for calling him Hog Man in my head. His name tag said Jerry.

He returned and started cleaning glasses. Marina and I looked around at the pictures on the walls.

"Oh!" Marina gasped. "That girl in the portrait!"

An old photo hung behind the bar—long black hair, dark eyes, porcelain skin. Her slight smile and the way she stared straight at you... gave me the creeps.

Jerry walked over. "That there was the daughter of one of the former mayors. Way back when. Before you two were born— hell, before I was born."

She looked too young in the photo. Definitely long gone now.

"She's pretty," Marina said.

"She was. They say she was murdered. Legend has it she walks the beaches at night, looking for the man who killed her. The weird part is, we've had a handful of unexplained crimes here—none of them ever solved. Men, all dead, strangled, and found lying on the shore. That's why I'm warning you two, since you're visiting, avoid going to the beach at night."

Okay. That got dark.

Marina sipped her water and almost choked.

"You alright?" Jerry asked. "Didn't scare you, did I?"

"No," Marina waved him off. "I'm fine."

"I'll get some napkins," Jerry said, heading to the back.

"What's the matter?" I asked her.

She held up a finger—signaling for me to wait.

Jerry returned with napkins. Perfect for my upcoming burger feast. A couple walked in, and he went over to greet them.

Marina leaned toward me.

"So you know how he said that girl's ghost can be seen walking the beach at night?"

"Yeah?"

"Well... Maeve snuck out last night. She told me this morning."

I kept listening.

"She said she saw someone—a girl—on the beach. Long dark hair covering her face. Glowing a little. Old nightgown. Dirty."

"You think it was her? The mayor's daughter?"

"I don't know," Marina said. "It's weird."

I stared down at the bar. I didn't have an answer. But the ghost tale was too strange to just ignore.

Marina got up and walked to the portrait. The name below it read: *Gladys Fitzgerald.*

"Gladys..." she whispered, coming back to sit next to me.

Jerry returned with my plate.

"Here you go, sir," he said, sliding it over.

"Thank you," I said.

It was a giant cheeseburger with melted cheese and seasoned fries—just like I hoped. But looking at it now... I didn't feel so hungry anymore.

Chapter Fifteen
Jude

"Where are you going?" Useless asked as I took the lead. We walked through town, and for the most part, she didn't say a word—except to politely greet the friendly old folks who passed by first.

I kept going, headed toward the edge of town where the woods started.

"I'm going into the forest," I said as we stopped at the entrance.

"But—Auri told us not to. He said stick to the outskirts, not the woods."

"Yeah? So?" I looked back at her, waiting for the point.

"So... we aren't supposed to go."

"Listen, Use—Daisy May, or whatever your name is—"

"It's Maeve."

I looked down at her. She was getting mad. Something I said triggered her, which only made me want to push more. It wasn't just to be a dick—though I was definitely being one. I wanted to see what kind of fight the weakest Veilkeeper of all time had in her.

She didn't back off. Didn't flinch. That surprised me.

"Okay, Maeve. Tell me one thing—if you're so scared to go into the woods, why did you even come here?"

She looked offended.

"What do you mean? I'm a Veilkeeper too. Just like you, Judy—or whatever your name is."

"It's Jude. And don't ever call me that shit again."

"Oh, so it's okay when you call me the wrong name?" she snapped, her voice rising. "What the fuck is your problem, anyway?"

I didn't expect her to go off like that. She'd been quiet until. This was getting interesting.

I laughed, smug as hell. "Look, Princess Daisy, I get that you're used to having assistants and handlers. People doing your missions for you. But I'm a real Veilkeeper. Not some play-pretend."

"I'm a real Veilkeeper too!" she snapped.

Gotcha, I thought.

"All right, then prove it," I said. "You think you've got what it takes? Prove it."

"Fine! I will!"

"Good."

Pause.

She looked around awkwardly. "Uh... how?"

"By fighting me. In the woods."

"What? But—" She glanced behind her at the tree line. "As a true Veilkeeper, I happen to follow Sir Aurelius's orders at all times. Therefore, I will not be going into those woods. He made it very clear we shouldn't go in without knowing the demon hotspots. We might walk right into a portal. That's gonna be a no for me, dog."

I laughed. "Wow."

She didn't look amused.

"Maeve, I didn't realize how scared you were. You really are a shrinking daisy."

"I'm what?"

"Shrinking next to me. I'm the stronger Keeper, and you're just a shrinking daisy. How about this—you stay here, and I'll go into the woods. I'll call you if I need someone to come sing a song."

She balled her fists. I knew that stance—Kayo does the same thing when I say something that pisses her off bad enough to make her want to slap me.

Maeve was mad. Like, really mad.

"You can't go in there, Jude," she said. "You might get killed."

Deep down, I knew she was right. But I kept my face composed like I didn't care.

"And then everyone will blame me," she added, looking down. "They'll ask why I didn't stop you."

"That's right, Maeve. And you can't stop me. Try if you want."

She started shaking a little. From stress. From the argument. From both. "I'm not going to fight you! I'm no match. Okay? We both know that you'd kick my ass. Not just because you're a guy, but because—you're stronger. I know that, all right?"

I scoffed and turned away. Waste of time.

"Where are you going?" she shouted after me. "Didn't you hear me?! JUDE!"

I kept walking. Ignored her.

Then I heard her sigh—and her footsteps trailing behind.

"Are you done being scared?" I asked without turning around.

"No. But I can't let you go die alone."

"That's noble."

"What can I say? Might be the only thing I contribute, right?"

"Probably." I didn't even try to hide how serious I was. "I still don't get why you didn't just send one of your people to help me with this case."

"That's why you're mad at me?" she asked. "Look I didn't have a choice. And what's so wrong with having team members?"

We kept walking. Trees overhead started blocking out the sun.

"Yeah, but I fight alongside mine. I don't just send them off like, 'Oh well, maybe they'll come back after doing my job for me.'"

She didn't say anything. I looked back—she still looked pissed. Arms crossed, walking behind me, stewing in it.

"Sometimes I don't have a choice," she finally said. "And I don't just send them off, Jude. They were fighting monsters long before I was even called to be a Keeper."

I didn't answer. Just walked deeper into the woods, scanning for energy. I felt something—faint, but evil.

"You feel that?" I asked.

"Huh? No. What?"

"There's something in here."

She stepped closer. Scared. Wow, even Kayo would handle this better. Kayo doesn't even fight, and she'd still be cooler under pressure than this.

I focused, just like Kosei taught me. I planted my feet and felt my surroundings.

Where is it... where... there.

I bolted in that direction.

"Wait, Jude! Don't leave me!" she yelled, running to catch up.

I didn't have time to babysit someone who was supposed to be on my level. I leapt over branches, ran through brush—pretty sure I jumped over a snake. No way Maeve was making it through all that.

But then—she was still behind me.

I stopped abruptly. She crashed into my back.

"Jude, what the hell—I almost got killed by a snake, I—"

"Shush," I warned. I was locked in.

I felt her hands grab my arm. But I didn't move. I was staring through the trees at something behind the limbs.

It was... tall. Pale. Sickly white. Like it hadn't seen sunlight in centuries. Long limbs. Hunched over. Taller than me if it stood up straight. Definitely a demon.

Maeve was shaking. I looked down—she was grabbing my arm and trembling hard.

I felt bad for a second. Then annoyed. *You're a Veilkeeper. You don't get to freak out at the sight of a demon!*

It hadn't noticed us yet.

Until it did.

It turned—and I saw human remains at its feet. It had been eating someone. *Fuck.*

It shrieked—sharp, alien, awful.

I broke from Maeve's grip and charged it.

"Jude, NO!" she cried.

It swung at me. Long arms. Claws out. I dodged and jumped. Big sharp teeth bared. One giant purple eye in the center of its lopsided skull.

Ugly as hell. Easily the nastiest one I've seen.

It looked at Maeve.

"Uh oh," she gulped.

"Maeve, run!" I shouted.

I summoned a ball of electric moon energy and hurled it. Missed—barely. It was too fast.

It charged her.

I chased it. Maeve tripped and fell over. The creature hovered over her about to attack, its mouth wide open.

Just before it sank its teeth into her, I leapt—slammed into it from behind and wrestled it down. We rolled in the dirt, teeth and claws flashing. I grabbed its head— snapped its neck.

One final squeal. Then silence.

I pushed its dead weight off me and stood. Maeve was walking toward me slowly, wide-eyed.

"Is it dead?" she asked.

"I think so." I stood up, brushing myself off. She offered her hand, but I didn't take it.

I looked around. No backup demons. For now.

I kicked it. Yep. Neck snap worked. This thing was strong—if it had caught Maeve, she'd be a goner.

At least we had answers now. People were disappearing because they were being eaten. And this demon definitely came from the other side. But which part of the

Demon World did it crawl out from? How many more like it were out there?

I pulled out my phone and took pictures. The demon. The body—or what was left of it. Too mangled to tell if it was a man, woman, or child.

This was messed up.

Maeve followed me in silence as I started walking back toward the edge of the woods.

"You should go home," I said under my breath—but loud enough for her to hear.

I heard her inhale sharply, but she didn't answer.

Maybe she knew I was right.

Whatever brought that thing here—or let it out—was worse. Stronger. Meaner.

And I needed real backup.

I needed Maeve and Marina on the first bus ride out of here.

Chapter Sixteen
Aurelius

My father, as serious as ever, looked me in the eyes, waiting for my response to the news he had just given me. From my right, I heard Gwen gasp, and in my peripheral vision, I saw her shaking. I hoped she would get that under control before he noticed.

He had a very strict rule: we are not to get attached to the Veilkeepers. No matter how long we've known them, we must remain neutral. Always. I used to be better at following that rule. But this group... made it hard.

I didn't want to endure the same punishment my sister Aurora did. And I think Gwen remembered that, because she quickly gulped and regained her composure. The news was just that shocking.

Though we'd suspected something based on our research into closing the alternate demon portal, those suspicions had now been confirmed.

"So... which one?" I asked, trying to sound unaffected. "Which Veilkeeper has to die for the portal to close?"

"We've called in reinforcements," Gwen said suddenly. "Caelum and Ryu are still on their way to Starbrook."

"Doesn't matter," I said, masking my reaction. "We already know the outcome."

"Yes," my father replied. "No matter who joins them, the instructions are clear. The only way to close this newly opened portal to the Demon World... is to sacrifice one of our own."

Again, I asked, "So which one?"

My father rubbed his chin and walked toward the tall glass windows that overlooked all of the Spirit World. The dark purple mist outside sometimes made it hard to see, but today the skies were clear. The light glared through the panes, and I told myself I'd blame the brightness if my eyes started to water.

"I had a feeling it would come to this," I said, watching him stare out the window. "This is why you had me send both Jude and Maeve."

He nodded.

"Father—Sir—if I may, Kosei is—"

"Kosei has been loyal for decades," my father interrupted. "Not just as a Veilkeeper, but as a trainer of warriors. His patience and temperament are rare. He can prepare the next Keeper once we find a replacement."

"Sir... Jude and Maeve are practically children. Nineteen and twenty. Wouldn't it make more sense to preserve our younger warriors?" Gwen asked.

"Another can replace them," he said calmly. "Kosei can train someone faster than those two ever could. I'd rather have one young Keeper alive and one seasoned Keeper who can train the next... than the alternative."

I tightened my jaw and nodded slowly, swallowing back the urge to argue. Gwen was standing beside me, clutching her chest, staring down at the floor like she was holding in a scream.

"You must understand," my father continued, "the seal might choose for us. It may not even matter what we decide. When the moment comes, there's a chance it will take whichever Keeper it wants. They don't have to fight each other. Fate will simply... be fate. As long as the portal is closed—and we find who opened it—that is all that matters."

"Very well, sir," I said, glancing down at the radar map I'd been given on arrival. "I'll return to the living world and complete the assignment. This visit has proven... useful. We now know how to solve the case."

That was a lie. We knew more about how to solve it— but this wasn't good news.

"Very well then, Prince Aurelius. I expect a full report in less than a week. I am hopeful this issue will be resolved soon."

He turned back to face me. I held his gaze.

"Agreed, sir," I said, bowing my head slightly.

"You may be excused."

He turned back to the window.

I turned quickly and walked out. I couldn't hold it in much longer. As I passed Gwen, I gently touched her arm—a silent cue to follow. She did.

We walked through the long corridor of the Spirit Castle without saying a word. Neither of us needed to speak. We knew exactly where to go. Where it was safe to talk. Where no one could hear us.

I could feel Gwen unraveling beside me, but she kept it together. Barely.

Every spirit we passed bowed as I walked through the halls. Their eyes followed us. I paced my steps until the crowd thinned, then sped up. Gwen matched me. When we reached the room, I opened the door and let her enter first. I shut it behind us and locked it.

She broke down the second she heard the latch click.

She covered her face and sobbed into her hands. I sat the radar map down on a nearby table and then moved to her. I wrapped my arms around her as she cried into my chest. My own eyes burned. But I didn't cry. Not yet.

"It's not fair," she choked. "This keeps getting harder every time."

"I know," I whispered.

I gave her the space. Let her cry. Because once we returned, we'd have to be strong again. We'd have to tell the group the truth.

Two things were now confirmed: a portal had opened... and it would require one of Earth's protectors to close. One of them had to die. No loopholes. No rewrites. Just death.

And I blamed myself.

I told them this was just a case. That a few demons had slipped through and I needed help tracking them down. They came willingly. With their whole lives ahead of them.

And now one of them wouldn't be going home.

Not because of a battle. Not because of bad luck. But because this was the cost.

I couldn't even decide who. Not that I would want to. I wasn't sure I'd survive choosing. I reached into my pocket and pulled out the talisman my father had given me today—the very one that would be used to summon the seal and close the portal. The tool that would require a sacrifice was in my hand. I squeezed it tightly, wanting to crush it as I thought about what this small thing was capable of. Then I shoved it back into my pocket.

Despite their constant disrespect—calling me Auri instead of Sir Aurelius—I cared about them. They were just kids when I first met them. Scared. Reckless. We got them through some awful fights. But this... this would be the hardest of them all.

Before, there was always a chance. A chance they'd live. A chance they could beat the odds.

This time, according to my father there didn't seem to be another way. No gamble. Just certainty.

One of my Veilkeepers was going to die.

I thought of suggesting Kosei. He was older. He'd lived. I knew if he heard the stakes, he'd trade places with either of them in a heartbeat—especially Jude. Although I also knew Jude would try to stop him.

I considered disobeying. Going to Kosei anyway before returning to Starbrook.

But my father was clear. Final.

I didn't have the authority to challenge him. Not now.

It was going to happen. And all I could do was figure out how to tell the rest of the team.

I stood there, holding Gwen. Thinking through every version of the conversation in my head. I debated not telling them at all. But that would be cruel. I couldn't do that to them.

They deserved to know.

They always knew there was a chance of death. But not like this. Not one hundred percent.

I wanted them to live as long as Kosei. I wanted them to outgrow this and get to the other side.

But I knew better. I knew life didn't care what we wanted.

Gwen finally pulled away and took a deep breath. I looked at her—her eyes wet, her face pale. I wiped a stray tear from her cheek and gently cupped her face.

Her big eyes met mine. She knew.

It was time.

I smiled faintly. She was so broken by this, because she cared for them too. If she could trade places, she would.

She took a step back, straightened her posture, and nodded.

"Okay," she said. "I'm ready to go now."

Chapter Seventeen
Jude

When I got back to the hotel, I went straight to the shower.

I got out and immediately felt annoyed—every single towel had been thrown on the floor.

Soren.

I was mad, but mostly about how the day had gone. The big ugly demon. Maeve running like a coward and almost getting her head bitten off. And now here I was, dripping wet, nothing to dry off with, laying bare-ass naked on my bed not giving a shit if Soren walked in. Honestly, that's what he gets for throwing all the towels around like this old-ass inn was going to send housekeeping. I've only seen that one dude at the front desk this whole time. If I wanted a clean towel, I'd probably have to go ask him—or just steal one from Auri, since he wanted us to report to his room soon anyway.

When Maeve and I got back to town, she apologized. Told me she was sorry for what happened.

I didn't say anything at the time but thinking back... yeah. She should be sorry.

She's letting everyone down. This Veilkeeper thing—it's rare. The world depends on us. And she's walking around like it's just some side gig. She needs to understand the weight of what she is. One way or another. I guess I'll be the one to make sure of it.

Then I remembered—I got to train with Kosei. His compound was only a one-hour train ride from where I lived. Maeve lived across the world, in the States. Maybe if she met Kosei... maybe she'd get it. Maybe she'd take it more seriously.

Once I was dry enough, I got dressed. Checked my phone. No missed calls from Kayo. Just a few texts from Soren and a video from my mom I didn't have time to open. I needed to get upstairs for the meeting.

The hallway and elevator were quiet. Too quiet. Something felt off. Like a weird energy was in the air, and I couldn't put my finger on it. I'll never forget how weird everything felt.

The elevator took forever, this time slower than usual. I rode it up a couple of floors. When the doors finally creaked open, I stepped out and walked to room 504. The door was cracked so I could enter.

I walked in.

Everyone was already there. Auri, Gwen—both looked... off. Gwen's eyes were sad. Almost like she'd been crying. Auri stood still, hands in his pockets, staring at the floor.

Maeve sat in the same place she had last time, closer to Auri. Marina and Soren were across from her, but

Marina wasn't even paying attention to him. She was focused entirely on Maeve.

I took a seat next to Maeve. "Jeez, who died?" I joked.

No one laughed. No one replied.

"Hello, Jude," Auri said, too soft. His tone sounded... different. Gentle.

"Hey," I responded, leaning forward, elbows on knees, right hand fidgeting with my left fingers. Everyone's weird energy was getting to me.

"Ready to start?" Auri asked Gwen.

She nodded, walked to the table behind me, and pulled out a radar map. I'd seen these before. Same type of device, just a different map.

"We've found two potential demon hotspots," Auri said, zooming in on one. "Here. And then... over here."

I leaned in, bumping into Maeve a little. Whatever. I was the one who actually had to fight the demons, so I needed to see the map more than she did.

"Ah, no way," I said. "Neither of those is where I fought that demon earlier."

"We'll get to that in a minute," Auri replied, his tone sharpening.

I looked at Maeve, I bet she already ratted me out. I saw her side-eye me, trying to act like she was focused on the map.

"These two locations," he continued. "One of them could be where the demon portal is."

"How do we know it's just one portal?" Marina asked.

"Good question," Auri replied. "According to Spirit

World analysts, there's only one portal. That's the only good news we've got."

"What?" I said, "There's bad news?"

Silence. Maeve stiffened next to me.

"Jude..." Auri started.

"Yeah? What?" I looked around. Everyone already knew something. I was the only one in the dark.

"We've received new information. And like I told Maeve, I want to be upfront with both of you. We now know how to close the portal."

"Okay, well... that actually sounds like good news. Better than your 'good news' from earlier, which was useless. If we can close one, we can close two." I laughed. "Right?"

The room went dead silent.

I could hear that sad little AC unit rattling in the corner.

Auri took a breath. Looked me straight in the eye. "Jude, in order to close the portal we must perform a ritual... it requires a sacrifice. One of Earth's protectors. A Veilkeeper."

Everyone stared at me.

I heard him. The words registered. But I just... didn't process them.

"Alright," I said, still squeezing my hand so tight my knuckles were going white. I'd loosen up. Then squeeze again. My mind still trying to process what Auri was saying.

"So... what does that mean?" I asked. I needed him to say it.

Gwen sniffled. Turned around and grabbed a tissue.

Maeve was frozen beside me. Tears in her eyes. Staring into nothing. Marina watched her like her heart was breaking.

Auri's voice didn't waver. "Jude, it means that in order to close the portal, you or Maeve will have to die. One of you. Your duty as a Veilkeeper will end. Permanently."

He said it like he was trying to make it sound noble. Like it was honorable. A sacrifice. Duty served.

I wasn't sure how to react. I looked up. Soren was staring at me too—his eyes full of something I didn't want to see.

Pity?

So I kicked into gear. My instincts. My wall.

"Alright," I said. "Okay—yeah. I mean... that's fate, right? We all knew this was part of the deal. Thought it'd be later in life, not now, but... okay."

I adjusted in my seat. Wiped the sweat from my palms onto my pants.

"Cool. So do you just stab one of us now, or what? How does it work?"

Maeve let out a choked sob. Marina got up and knelt in front of her. Gwen rushed over to rub her back.

I rolled my eyes. "What'd I say?"

"I don't know how it happens," Auri said. "The portal might choose. I'm not even sure how it selects or when."

"Then doesn't that mean— can't we find another way to close the thing?" Soren asked.

Auri looked at him. "We're researching alternatives. But right now... this is all we have."

"But there are other ways, right? There must be."

Marina asked, her voice desperate as she held Maeve tighter.

Auri didn't answer.

That silence said everything.

We were screwed. One of us was going to die.

The room fell quiet. Marina crying. Gwen crying. Maeve silent but shattered. Soren zoned out, eyes wet. Auri deep in thought.

And me?

Just sitting there. Watching them all. Numb.

"I killed a demon today," I finally said.

"I heard," Auri replied. "After I told you not to go into the woods."

I pulled out my phone and handed it over. "Here. This is what it looked like."

Gwen leaned over his shoulder to see. Auri turned the phone to Marina. She shook her head.

"What?" I asked.

"Sorry—it's just... I've never seen one like this," she said. "I don't even know what kind it is."

"They must be coming from an unknown part of the Apparition World," Marina added. "Maybe my brother will recognize them."

"Maybe," Auri echoed, forwarding the photos and handing my phone back.

As I took it, I asked, "Speaking of Ryu, when is he getting here? I thought you said they were on the way."

"Soon," Auri said, leaning back and rubbing his head. He looked like hell.

I didn't accept the news. Couldn't.

I'd already killed one demon. There had to be another way. There had to be.

I refused to believe this was it.

Ryu and Caelum were coming. They'd fix it. No one was going to die.

I kept repeating that to myself.

I'm not going to die.

I will have help.

I'm not going to die.

I caught myself rocking slightly in my seat. I don't think the others noticed. I stiffened up trying to remain cool, calm, and collective. But inside I was starting to panic. I just kept thinking the same thoughts over and over to help keep my controlled demeanor intact.

I'm not going to die. I'm not going to die.

I'm not going to die.

Chapter Eighteen
Maeve

I sat with my favorite notepad, writing a few lines of poetry—my private way of processing things. Right now, I felt everything all at once.

Doubt.

Doubt in Aurelius. Doubt in everything he'd told me. Doubt that he ever really cared. And uncertainty—so much of it. About what was coming, about what this all meant. There was too much unknown. It scared me.

And grief. I wasn't even sure if it was grief for myself, or maybe for Jude—the guy who clearly didn't like me but still saved my life. As cruel as he'd been, he could've let me die today. He could've let that thing rip my head clean off my shoulders. It was right behind me, and if Jude had been even a second too late, I wouldn't be sitting on this balcony, listening to the ocean. I'd be gone. And maybe a new Veilkeeper would be summoned to take my place.

Even though Auri himself wasn't sure that's how it worked.

But still—Jude may have had a chance to work with someone stronger. Someone not... useless. Like he called me.

I closed my notepad and clutched it tight.

I kept thinking about the portal. About what was said to is in that heavy meeting in Auri's room. I was so overwhelmed I didn't catch all of it, but Marina explained it later: it wasn't the portal that needed a Veilkeeper in order to close—it was the seal. The seal required a life.

That meant me. Or Kosei. Or Jude.

These new details made everything worse.

I considered calling Orpheus. He's a powerful sorcerer. Maybe, just maybe, he and Cleo—and her sisters Leslie and Este, who also practiced magic—could find another way. But Marina said even if they could temporarily close the portal, without sealing it, it would just reopen. All it would take is the wrong demon. And according to Auri, his father—King Aurelius—*wanted* it sealed this way. The way that costs a life.

Being a Veilkeeper sometimes felt like working for a corporation that doesn't care about its employees. The moment one of us dies, they're already looking for a replacement.

I knew King Aurelius didn't care about us. Not even when we were little kids.

But sometimes I wondered about Auri. And Gwen.

Did they really care? Or were they just good at pretending?

Marina poked her head out the balcony door. "I'm going to bed."

I smiled, pretending everything was fine. "Okay."

She looked out at the ocean, then back at me. "No late-night strolls, you hear me?"

I laughed. "Hell no. Not after what you told me about ghost girl." Not to mention the demon I saw today. I didn't want to run into any of his friends. I didn't even want to say it out loud. Acknowledging it made it more real.

But I *was* thinking about ghost girl. *Gladys*, apparently. I wanted to go to that restaurant and see the picture for myself. Was she connected to all of this?

Auri had told us before Jude arrived that he didn't think so. Said if it *was* Gladys, she was just a wandering spirit—either lost, or one who *chose* to remain. I didn't understand that part. Chose to? Why would someone choose that?

I stood and grabbed the balcony railing, looking down the beach where I'd seen her the night before. It was around the same time. I hoped maybe I'd catch another glimpse of her.

But there was no one there.

Except—Auri.

He was standing on the small bridge that led from the inn down to the beach. Hands in his pockets, watching the shoreline.

I wondered if he was looking for the ghost too. Part of me pictured Gladys seeing him and thinking, *"No way you're dragging me to the Spirit World."*

I ran back into the room. I wanted to talk to Auri—alone. As I passed Marina's bed, she was still sitting up, reading.

"Where do you think you're going?" she asked, side-eyeing me.

"I want to talk to Auri," I said. "I'll be right back."

"Okay," she said with that *I'm choosing to believe you* tone.

I slipped out and jogged down the stairwell. Pushed through the stubborn door that led to the beach. He was still on the bridge, his hair shifting in the breeze. The wind wasn't nearly as aggressive as last night.

"Auri," I called out.

He turned, blank-faced. "Maeve."

I reached the bridge and looked up at him. He looked tired.

"Sorry. You probably don't want to talk."

"It's fine," he said. "What do you need?"

That tone—cold, detached. It stung.

What *did* I need? I'd known him half my life. He used to always look out for me. But tonight, he seemed distant. Like he'd already started pulling away. Like he knew one of us wasn't going to make it, and he was already preparing for that.

I didn't want to ask about death.

"I was wondering... Jude's friends—are they as powerful as Orpheus and Dante?"

"Just as, if not a bit more," he said.

"Is that why you chose them? Instead of bringing members from my team?"

He paused. Shook his head. "There's a reason. I needed Orpheus and the others to be a second wave—backup in case things go south. They're geographically closer. If we fail... they'll get here faster. It wasn't personal."

"Oh no," I said quickly. "I'm not offended. It's okay."

"It's *not* okay," he said suddenly, turning away and leaning against the wooden railing, his head hanging low. "None of this is okay."

There he was. *That* was the Auri I knew.

I walked over and placed a hand on his back. I'd never had to comfort him before. But then he stood up straight again, like he was reminding himself to stay strong. I backed off.

He looked into my eyes.

"Maeve, I'm proud of you."

That surprised me. "Wait... really?"

"You've come so far. I remember when we first met you—it was on a beach, wasn't it? This same ocean, just a different beach."

"Myrtle Beach," I said. "All those years ago."

He nodded. "You've grown into this beautiful, unstoppable force. And now... they expect me to sit back and let you wither away."

His voice cracked with anger.

I looked down, ashamed. "I'm not unstoppable, Auri. You heard what happened today. I ran. I held Jude back."

He was quiet. Then shook his head and shoved his hands in his pockets. "You're strong. You just haven't awakened your power again. You still have it. You're just... afraid. And that fear is what's holding you back. It's blocking your moon energy. But I know what you're capable of."

I almost cried. He *did* believe in me.

I thought back—there *were* times I saved us. Times I fought hard. I had power. And I'd forgotten that.

"No more running," I said, voice steady. "Got it."

He smiled, but it faded quickly. Like another thought crept in—something painful. Maybe it was the reality that even if I awakened all my power, it might not matter.

One of us would still have to die.

"I think Jude hates me," I said, changing the subject.

Auri actually laughed. "He doesn't."

"I wouldn't blame him."

"He's always been a little shithead," Auri said, a touch of humor in his voice. "But once you get to know him... he's loyal. A true friend."

His voice cracked again. Just slightly.

He really cared about Jude, I could tell.

"Are his friends like him?" I asked. "Are they... nicer?"

Auri didn't answer that part. Which wasn't very reassuring.

Instead, he said, "Jude is nice. He just has someone waiting for him. He doesn't want to die. And that fear... it comes out as arrogance."

"I didn't know," I said.

We stood there in silence. Listening to the waves crash against the shore.

And for the first time that night, I felt a little better after talking with Auri.

I knew it wouldn't last. But I'd take it—for now.

Chapter Nineteen
Soren

Marina and I sat outside the inn on the old, rustic, white-painted chairs—she called them that—like the kind you'd find abandoned in a garden somewhere. Except we weren't in a garden. We were posted near the entrance of the inn, easy to find in case Jude and Maeve wanted to join us.

Jude had been trying to call Kayo all morning. He was beside himself when he woke up. I guess that tough guy front he put on during last night's meeting had officially worn off.

Marina said Maeve had gone to bed late and had trouble sleeping, so she was still out.

"It's probably a good idea," Marina told me, biting into her bagel with cream cheese. "No need to rush her into waking back up to this reality. Let her escape for a bit longer."

Even with cream cheese on her lip, she still looked beautiful. I tried not to stare.

It was clear to both of us what our roles were now.

There was no way in hell we were just going to accept that Jude or Maeve was supposed to die. Not happenin'. Jude might've been a pain in the ass, but he was like a brother to me. We grew up together. I would die before I let anything happen to him.

And I sure as hell wasn't going to let Maeve die either. That would destroy Marina, and I couldn't handle watching that happen to her. There *had* to be another way—and we were going to find it.

A part of me didn't trust that Spirit World was actually doing all it could to find that "other way," like Aurelius and Gwen promised. Spirit World made it pretty clear over the years that Veilkeepers were disposable to them. Why would they waste time finding a second solution when they already had one that involved one of them dying?

Marina agreed. But we weren't about to tell Jude or Maeve that theory.

It wasn't that I thought Auri and Gwen were lying. I think they genuinely wanted to believe the researchers were looking into alternatives. Gwen was up all-night reading about seals. Auri too. They *cared*. That much was obvious.

"I feel like I'm going to have scabies when I leave this place," I joked.

Marina laughed. "That bad, huh?"

"Well yeah, after I saw those towels—" I started, then remembered she was still eating. Didn't seem to bother her, though. She kept looking at me with those big maroon eyes, just waiting for me to continue talking.

"Ever since the towel incident, I've been cautious about everything in this place."

"Smart," she said, brushing crumbs from her hands after finishing her bagel. I'd already eaten mine.

"So... the guys are supposedly close," I said, bringing up Caelum and her punk-ass brother Ryu. Not that I'd ever call him that out loud. Not because I was afraid—but because I was trying to be respectful. For Marina.

"Aren't you just so excited to see my brother again?" she teased.

I rolled my eyes. "I'm over the moon. Just giddy with joy. Nothing would make my day more."

Ryu had always rubbed me the wrong way. He acted like he was too good for everything. People would talk to him, and he'd just ignore them. He respected Jude, though. Of course. Everyone respects Jude. When we first met Ryu, he was... well, not exactly evil, but definitely leaning that way.

Jude was actually assigned to investigate him once. I don't think Ryu was out there trying to *kill* humans, but he didn't seem to lose sleep over dead ones either.

Now he's part of our team. I think he only does it because Auri makes him. The minute he's off the hook, I bet he disappears. He's just that kind of guy. And honestly, I *hate* him. But I'd never say that in front of Marina.

They're opposites. Light and dark. Water and fire. Obviously.

I was excited about Caelum coming, though. He was cool. We went way back—even before Jude worked with him on a case. Caelum used to be a full-on demon in a past life, but now he's a reincarnated human who can still tap into his demon energy somehow. No clue how that works. He'd have to explain. But yeah—Caelum? Solid dude. Not like Ryu.

"Have you worked with my brother recently?" Marina asked.

"Uh..." I leaned back in my chair, thinking about that time almost a year ago. Auri split us into pairs during a mission in some underground tunnels. Of course, I got stuck with Ryu.

There were two paths to the exit. Did he talk to me about which one to take? Nope. Just picked one and started walking.

Then—boom. A giant-ass boulder fell from the ceiling. Straight out of a movie or some horror video game. There was nowhere to run but forward, and Ryu, with his freaky demon speed, just took off. Left me behind.

I ran for my life. Barely made it out, thanks to training with Jude and Kosei. When I finally got through, panting and soaked in sweat, I swear I saw that smug bastard laughing at me.

Marina would *never* do that. Like I said—they're nothing alike.

I snapped back to reality. Marina was still waiting for an answer.

"Yeah, we worked together," I said. "And he was... well, him."

She didn't seem offended. "My brother can be cold. I know."

Cold? That was an understatement. That dude was Antarctica in human form.

"He's hard to get to know," she continued. "But he has come through. I'm looking forward to seeing him again. And honestly? I'm not looking forward to much else right now."

I could see the sadness creeping up on her again. I stayed quiet, letting her talk. Letting her feel safe.

"You know, I sometimes wonder why he's the way he is," she said. "I blame our dad walking out when we were little. Ryu never got along with him, even when he *was* around. And when he died... Ryu didn't seem to care. He left home against our mom's wishes and never looked back."

"Wow," I said. I didn't care what turned Ryu into an asshole, but I kept my mouth shut and listened. Marina needed to talk.

"He came to save me when I was kidnapped and brought to the human world," she added. "That's how I know he's capable of love. Somewhere, buried deep."

I bit back my usual sarcastic response. Just nodded.

She smiled. Like she knew exactly what I was thinking and found it funny.

"Anyway," she said, sliding her chair back. "They'll be here soon. That probably means another meeting with Aurelius and the others. Let's go make ourselves useful. Do some research. Maybe we'll figure out more than we know right now."

I smiled and stood, following her lead. Marina had a way about her—like everything would be okay, even when nothing really was. No wonder Maeve felt safer with her around.

I wasn't going to let anything happen to any of them. Not Maeve. Not Jude. Especially not Marina.

We headed off to do some research. Not even sure where to begin—but I'd figure it out. For them.

Chapter Twenty
Maeve

Everyone spent the day researching. Auri and Gwen brought a stack of books. Not sure where they were from, but it made me wonder if they were from the Spirit Realm. Why did we have them and not the supposed research team?

That's because it was becoming more and more clear —without it being said out loud—that now we *were* the research team. Everyone read and brainstormed in Auri's room. I excused myself around eight that night, saying I was going to rest. It was a lie.

Thankfully, Marina didn't offer to follow me.

Being cooped up in that room, spending what might be my last few days—or hours—alive just sitting there wasn't how I wanted to go. I decided to go back to my room, grab my fake ID, and head to one of the small pubs outside the inn.

Thing is, I wasn't really a drinker. I had no idea what to order, but since I was probably going to die anyway, I didn't care. I threw on some sweats over my clothes because the wind gets chilly at night here, and I added a baseball cap.

I exited the hotel. The guy at the front desk—can't remember his name—was already gone for the evening. I half expected Auri, Gwen, or Marina to pop out and ask, "And where do you think you're going?"

But I guess they were too distracted with trying to find another way to close the portal.

I walked down the street a little, head down, my hair and hat shielding my face. I tried not to look suspicious. Being that I was a visitor and this town's population was, like, negative three, anyone who passed me stared. I walked into the restaurant bar where Marina said she saw the picture of the ghost girl Gladys—the one that walks the beach. As soon as I stepped inside and looked left— bam. Big glowing creepy picture of Gladys. Even weirder than Marina described. It really did feel like her eyes followed you.

The bar was surprisingly crowded. A lot of men, a few women with smoker voices, all in their fifties or older. There were a few younger guys too. Everyone was talking about fishing.

I sat alone at the end of the bar and kept to myself. The bartender, a big guy named Jerry according to his name tag, approached me.

"What can I get you?" he asked without even asking for my ID. (Which wasn't real and had a fake name on it. I know—I know. Bad.)

"Uh—beer," I said, unsure.

Jerry limped away without asking what kind or size.

He came back and slid a tall glass to me like a professional. It only spilled a little.

"Start a tab?" he asked.

"No thank you," I said. I planned to pay cash. I sat there alone, just taking in the place. The lights were dim. The people were loud and drunk, giving each other a hard time, telling stories. All I could think about was how these people were so small-town. And they didn't seem to mind. This small, tiny restaurant was enough for them. These were their Friday night plans every week. They probably never seen the lights of a big city—and they were content.

I wondered what that would be like. Growing up somewhere like this, falling in love with a fisherman, raising a family, dying a simple person—but happy.

The truth was, behind all the glitter and glamour, I felt no glory. I felt shallow. Empty. Marina was all I had. And she was enough, but sometimes, I wanted more. I yearned for more. I was always singing cheesy pop songs about love, but I'd never even experienced it firsthand. I wanted to—badly. But now it looked like I'd never get the chance.

My parents always chased off or scared away any guy I showed interest in. They would tell me "He's not good enough for you," or "He just wants your money."

Another thing I wasn't ready to say out loud: I was a virgin. Never have I ever.

My parents would've lost their minds if I ever lost my virginity. They expected me to wait until marriage. Once, when I was fifteen and they found out I kissed a boy, I was punished. My mom held me down on the carpet while my dad screamed in my face. They still expected me to write love songs but never experience love. The truth was, I hated them sometimes.

I never had thoughts like this before, but after almost getting my head eaten off by that skin walker-looking thing, I was starting to look at life differently. I had to put my life in the hands of a stranger—a stranger who didn't even like me that much: Jude.

Before, I'd never truly feared dying on a mission. Orpheus or Auri always made me feel safe—protected, somehow. Even when the danger was real, I didn't think I'd actually die.

This time felt different. I could feel my own mortality.

I glanced at the Gladys portrait again. Her eyes weren't on me anymore. Weird.

They were locked on a table of men in the corner. I turned, and—oops—accidentally made eye contact with one of them. *Oh no.*

He got up and started walking over. Tall, dark-haired, wearing a hat. Looked like he'd just gotten off work. I turned back around quickly, but it was too late. He was approaching fast. And then it hit me—he was kind of cute. And there was a chance I might die tomorrow. Maybe I should go for it?

My eyes widened at my own thoughts, but I tried to calm myself. I looked up again—he was standing right next to me.

"Why do I feel like I know you from somewhere?" he asked. I wasn't sure if it was a pick-up line, small talk, or if he actually recognized me.

"I get that a lot," I said.

"No kidding. You look like someone—I just can't remember her name." He leaned against the counter.

I hoped he wouldn't figure it out and blow my cover. He looked like he was in his thirties. A little too old for what I had in mind. I decided to scrap the whole idea.

Jerry limped over. "You need another one, Brad?"

Ew. Brad. No thanks. I wasn't going to lose my virginity to a guy like him. Nuh-uh.

"Yeah, another round for the group back there," he said, pulling out his wallet like he wanted me to see it.

"So, what's a girl like you doing in here alone?"

So original. I sipped my beer, gripping the glass.

"Who says I'm alone?" I asked.

"Uh, you've been sitting in this corner by yourself."

I sipped again. "And you've been watching me?"

"You're kind of hard to miss in a place like this. Hat and all—you still stick out like a sore thumb."

What did he mean by "and all"? I wondered.

"You can come join us over there. We don't bite. Just some fishermen exchanging stories. Exciting stuff."

"Uh—" I stalled.

"Well, you think about it," he said.

Then, out of nowhere, another guy walked up. I hadn't even seen him approach. Younger. Light brown hair. "This guy bothering you?" he asked.

Brad rolled his eyes. "Travis, the hell? I'm not bothering her. Just asking if she wanted to come sit with us."

"You'll have to excuse him," Travis said. "He doesn't know how to read a room."

Brad turned to Travis. "What do you mean? You just

met me. Only been here a week and already acting like you run the place."

Travis laughed. He was better looking than Brad.

The beer was starting to kick in. That's probably the only reason I tolerated them. They were both trying to impress me, but I wasn't interested in either of them.

"I'm Travis," he said, reaching out his hand.

I couldn't remember what name was on my fake ID. I went with the first thing that came to mind. "Gladys," I said.

Travis pushed Brad out of the way and took the seat next to me. Brad didn't seem to care. Jerry was already delivering beers to Brad's table.

"So, you've been here a week?" I asked.

"That's right," he said. "What brings you here, Gladys?"

"I, uh..." *Think of a lie.* "I have family in the area."

Travis raised an eyebrow. "Random."

"Yeah, I know. My aunt moved here when she got married."

"I might know her. What's her name?"

I stalled and took a big gulp of beer. "Why would I tell you that? You're a stranger."

"I mean... I don't see why not. You told me your name."

Haha. If only he knew.

We talked for a while. He told me he was apprenticing with a fisherman. I wasn't really listening. The conversation was so boring.

"I'll be back," he said and headed toward the bathroom.

Perfect. Time to leave. I'd already paid. I turned to go but saw Gladys's eyes staring again. *Holy shit.* Maybe it was the beer.

I turned again—here comes Brad, stumbling.

"I know now," he said. "I know where I've seen you. You look like that one girl on TV."

I smiled, fake as hell. "That's crazy."

"You're not her, though. You're way prettier."

Ugh. I scanned for a way out. Then Travis came back.

"Brad, chill. Go sit down."

"Doesn't she look like that flower girl on TV?"

My heart rate spiked. Were they about to figure me out?

"Flower girl?" Travis asked. "Brad, you're drunk. Go sit down before you hurt yourself."

Brad stared a moment longer, then shuffled off.

"I better go," I said.

"I'll walk you," Travis offered.

"No, that's okay."

"I don't mind. Besides, you picked a bad time to visit your aunt."

He held the door as we exited.

"Bad time?"

"Haven't you heard the rumors? People are going missing. A lot of fishermen have left because of it. Only the brave stuck around."

"Missing?"

"Yep." He said it like he was amused.

I backed away slightly. "Oh."

"Yeah, they just vanish. Been going on a while. Crazy, huh?"

"If you knew about it, why come here?"

"I—I'm in training," he said, fumbling. Something about him felt off.

"I guess my aunt didn't want me to know," I replied. "Anyway, I really need to go."

"I'll walk you."

"No, really, I'm fine."

"It's no big deal," he said, stepping closer.

"You're not listening," I snapped.

"Alright, alright," he said, smirking.

I turned and walked away quickly, praying he wouldn't follow me. But I felt him behind me. I turned.

"Dude."

"What? I'm headed this way. Coincidence, I swear."

Was he staying at the same inn? There were only a couple others down past it.

I said nothing. Just kept walking. I caught his reflection in a window—still there. Still smiling.

What the hell?

Thankfully, I spotted Auri and Marina outside. Auri tapped her arm. I jogged to them.

"There you are!" Marina said. "Where have you been? We told you—no strolls!"

"I went to the bar. This creepy guy—" I turned to point, but Travis was gone.

"Oh."

"Creepy guy?" Auri asked.

"He was right there. Don't tell me he was a ghost too."

"Maybe," Auri said, hands on his hips.

"He talked to people. He can't be a ghost."

"I saw him," Marina said. "He ran through the alley when he saw us. Looks like he headed for the beach. He was following you?"

I nodded.

"Forget him," Auri said. "Just some desperate creep. We'll keep an eye out. But stop wandering off."

I sighed. This place sucked.

Auri spoke again. "In other news, we may have figured out an alternative plan. Maybe."

I looked at Marina—she nodded excitedly.

"That's great," I said. "I think? You said 'maybe.'"

"We're not certain," Auri replied.

"Still better than nothing," Marina added. "We might be on to something."

"You're this happy over a maybe?" I asked.

"There's one more thing we came to tell you." Marina grinned.

"What?" I asked, looking between them.

"They're here," she said. "My brother is here."

Chapter Twenty-One
Marina

I could tell Maeve was drunk off the one beer she *claimed* to have had. She was staggering all over the place. I grabbed her arm to walk with her. I thought I got rid of all her fake IDs, but apparently not. I'd definitely be taking this one.

We walked through the lobby with Aurelius.

My brother and the others were out on the main deck, behind the building where the pool still had a giant tarp over it—even though it was technically vacation season. I guess they figured, why even bother opening the pool? It's not like anyone would come here. After being here only a short time, I couldn't imagine anyone in their right mind wanting to stay at this place—unless they were specifically looking for solitude.

We stepped outside, Auri leading the way. I saw the group standing by the covered pool. There was just enough lighting from the old deck lamps.

Soren, Gwen, and Jude stood together, while my

brother Ryu and their friend Caelum were in front of them. I approached, still holding Maeve's arm.

"Hello," Caelum greeted with his usual friendliness. He was tall like Soren, maybe a little leaner. He had a small faded scar under his left eye and cherry red hair. His cool gray eyes scanned us, keeping a warm expression as we got closer. He reached out a hand to Maeve.

"It's so nice to meet you, Ms. Maeve. I'm Caelum."

Maeve smiled big. I couldn't tell if she knew which guy was my brother. She shook his hand. "Nice to meet you, Mr. Caelum. Thank you for being so nice," she blurted, clearly taking a shot at Jude.

Jude stiffened and looked away. We all laughed a little.

Caelum was polite, sweet as ever.

My brother, on the other hand, stood with his hands in his pockets. He was a little shorter than the other guys. Dressed in all black. Same eyes as me—big and maroon— but his were always narrowed, like he was annoyed. That was just his face.

I walked up to him. He didn't move or greet me, so I spoke first. "Ryu, it's good to see you."

No hug, no nothing. Just a nod.

Maeve picked up on his vibe immediately and stepped behind me.

"This is Maeve," I said. "I believe you two are the only ones here who don't know each other."

Maeve stepped forward, trying to be polite. She looked up at him— "Hi," she said softly.

He blinked once and gave her another silent nod.

Classic Ryu. He didn't *mean* to come off like an ass—

well, Soren might say otherwise—but he'd been this way since we were kids.

"Alright, I'm glad we've all met," Auri said. "Shall we head inside?"

We went into the lobby since the front desk guy, was long gone. Everyone took their seats. Maeve kept staring at Ryu. I noticed. And I *know* he noticed too. She was more than likely trying to see the resemblance between us. He grimaced and rolled his eyes a little.

He definitely stuck out here. Pale skin from being a total night owl. The townspeople were gonna stare hard if they saw him.

He sat on the arm of the couch, hands still in his pockets, eyes on Auri. Maeve sat on the cushion beside me—too close for comfort. I sat in the middle, with Soren on my left. Jude and Caelum stood nearby, catching up with their usual bro-handshake. Jude was even smiling. First genuine smile I'd seen from him since we got here. Maybe because his team was finally complete.

Gwen and Auri were on the opposite couch, with Ryu on the end.

"Alright," Auri began. "We did a quick scan of the research books—"

"From ye olden times," Gwen joked. "A lot of it had to be translated."

"Right," Auri continued. "Gwen and I already got Ryu and Caelum up to speed. Today we discovered something that was overlooked in the texts."

"Hurry up, jeez," Jude cut in, arms crossed. "The suspense is *literally* killing me."

"And me," Maeve slurred. No way she would've spoken up if she hadn't had that beer.

Jude shook his head.

"We aren't sure yet," Auri went on. "As Gwen said, we're still translating. Originally, we assumed the seal required the *soul* of a Veilkeeper. But after translating these texts in their many forms... nowhere did we find anything about a soul."

"Well, that's good, right?" Maeve asked a little too loudly. I nudged her to let him finish.

"However, we did translate some of the text, and we believe it says—the seal will require the *blood* of a Veilkeeper."

Silence.

"Uh... yay?" Jude asked, deadpan. "How is that any better?"

"Yeah, really," Soren added.

"How much blood?" I asked the question we all didn't want to know but needed answered.

"We assume... all of it," Auri said. "Enough to kill the person being sacrificed."

Another long silence.

"Again," Jude said, "how is this better?"

"It *is* better!" Gwen insisted.

"How?" Jude asked. "No, really—how?"

"Oh, I get it," Caelum spoke up. "It *is* better. Because there are *two* of them."

"Huh?" Jude said, looking between Maeve and Auri.

"We're thinking both of you can donate a large portion of blood. Not enough to kill either of you. Just enough to seal it."

"And we'll have medical supplies on site," Gwen added. "I just need your blood types."

"Who the fuck came up with this shit?" Jude muttered.

No one answered.

"No really, this sounds like a bad plot of some dark horror movie. What twisted weirdo said, 'Let's close the portal with *blood*?'"

"We assume one of the demon gods from long ago," Auri replied. "Look, it's not ideal. We don't even know if it'll work."

"Wait," I cut in, "weren't you told the seal would likely choose which Veilkeeper it wanted to take?"

"That's another thing we learned today," Auri said, and I could hear the frustration in his voice. "Nowhere in the text did it say that. It appears...maybe that was something my father made up."

"Why would he do that?" Soren asked.

Auri sighed. "I've told you—when it comes to King Aurelius, he doesn't exactly have the Veilkeepers' best interest at heart."

"More like doesn't give a damn," I muttered.

"Try not to take it personally," Auri added. "He's always been this way."

"King Aurelius was hoping that once Maeve and Jude made it to the seal," Gwen explained, "one would turn on the other."

"What?" Jude asked.

"Yes. Think about it. The seal won't just activate and take a Veilkeeper's life. Someone would have to perform the ritual and make the sacrifice for it to work."

"Oh," Jude said flatly. "So, he's banking on desperation. One of us killing the other."

Gwen looked at Auri. He nodded.

"Yep. Appears so."

"Well, at least you're telling them," Soren added. "You could've let your dad's plan play out and Maeve would be dead."

"Hey!" I snapped.

"Oh sorry, but it's true," Soren replied.

"I think that's my *hey!*" Jude shot back. "How do *you* know Maeve wouldn't be the one to back-stab me?"

"Because... well she seems nice and you're kind of a jerk," Soren shrugged.

Jude looked like he was going to grab him, but Gwen stepped in.

"Boys. Not now!" she hissed.

"So, I guess in a way... this is good news?" I tried to piece it together.

"Yes," Auri nodded. "If we get the blood supplies, manage the blood loss, and keep demons away—we might seal it without losing anyone. *Might.*"

I looked at Maeve, who was oddly quiet.

"Maeve? Anything to add?" I asked.

"Any thoughts, sweetheart?" Gwen chimed in.

Maeve looked up—her eyes back on Ryu. "Yeah," she said slowly, pointing at him. "I *really* want to know what he sounds like when he talks."

I quickly grabbed her hand and pulled it down.

Soren burst out laughing.

"Okay, meeting adjourned," Jude said, heading for the stairs.

Caelum smiled. Gwen handed him a keycard and gave him a quick hug before he followed Jude off.

She handed Ryu his keycard too. No *thank-you* from him, of course.

"Goodnight, everyone," Auri and Gwen said, heading toward the elevators.

That left me, Soren, Maeve, and Ryu.

Soren peeked over at Ryu's room number on his card. "Ah man, your room's next to mine. Come on. Goodnight, ladies." Soren said before they walked off.

Once they were in the stairwell, I turned to Maeve.

"Girl, are you okay?" I giggled.

"Huh?" she said, eyes glazed.

"Yeah, let's get you to bed," I said, guiding her toward the stairs. "That was a lot."

"Which part?" she asked.

"The *whole* thing. All of it."

Chapter Twenty-Two
Maeve

That was so embarrassing! I thought to myself the next morning, replaying how meeting Caelum and Marina's twin brother Ryu went down.

"He thinks I'm so cringey," I groaned, burying my face in a pillow.

"It's fine," Marina giggled from her side of the room. She was folding our clothes, separating what was clean from what needed to be washed. "I'm sure he's not thinking much about you at all."

I lifted my head and glared at her over the pillow.

"No offense," she added quickly.

I smacked myself in the face with the pillow and screamed into it. "UGH!"

She kept folding. She was used to my dramatic outbursts.

"That is not how I pictured meeting your brother," I muttered, tossing the pillow aside. "He wouldn't even talk to me. He probably thinks I'm a loser that can't fight so he had to come all the way here. And there's no telling what Jude's already said to make me look worse."

"I promise you, that's not it. I knew he'd be like that. Honestly, I'd be more surprised if he *had* spoken to you." Marina defended, "Ryu's never been a man of many words. He's more of a thinker than a speaker."

I paused, considering that. I guess it was refreshing to have someone like that around. The silent observer, maybe catching things the rest of us miss. Still, I couldn't help but take it personally. He didn't say anything, so I assumed he didn't like me.

"Also... last night?" Marina asked.

"I think you imagined it," I lied, then confessed. "Okay, maybe. I was drunk."

"Speaking of drunk—" she tossed a shirt at my face, "—how many drinks did you really have last night?"

"One," I said quickly. She arched an eyebrow. "One big, tall... one."

"So basically two or three beers in one giant glass."

I gave her a tight, guilty smile.

She shook her head. "No more of that. Hand it over."

"What?"

"Your fake ID. Cough it up."

I sighed, reached into my pillowcase, and slapped it into her hand.

She snatched it away. "Thank you. And this *better* be the only one."

"It is. Jace got it for me," I muttered.

"Well, when we get back to Rhode Island, I'm going to have a long talk with Jace."

"You mean *when you* get back." I looked out the glass balcony door.

She walked over and sat beside me on the bed. "Hey, listen. They're finding other plans. Last night's meeting was a bit... gory and not ideal, but I think we might be onto something. It's going to work out."

"A bit gory?" I raised a brow.

"Well, the idea that you and Jude basically have to bleed out into a seal is... yeah."

"We don't even know if it'll work," I interrupted. "What if it rejects both of us because it only wants one? What if the translation is wrong? They still didn't sound too sure of anything."

"That's—" she paused, "you're thinking worst-case scenario."

"I *have* to. We're in a worst-case scenario. So, excuse me for having one—or three—beers disguised as one. I could die today, Marina. *Today.* Maybe."

"Don't say that," she snapped.

"I might."

"You won't," she said sharply. "I won't let it happen."

We went quiet. She stared down at the floor.

"You can't stop it," I whispered.

"I can make a choice too," she said quietly. I knew what she meant.

"You can't do that," I said, thinking of Jude.

Marina looked up. Her demon eyes were glowing red today instead of their usual maroon. "I can if I have to. I'm not going to let you die."

It shocked me. Marina was the gentlest person I knew. A healer, never violent. But she was a demon. If she had to be brutal, she could be. The idea that she'd already made her choice scared me. Jude had his team—Soren, Caelum, even Ryu. They'd been together for years. They were stronger than us.

What if they were thinking the same thing Marina was... except I was the one they'd let die?

The thought of running away crossed my mind. Let Jude deal with it alone. But Auri and Gwen would track me down. I'd lose all their respect, and the choice would become obvious. Why keep a cowardly, runaway Veilkeeper around? No, there was no running.

I had to tap back into my power. Fast. I had to work with Jude—but also watch him. Because if it came down to it, Marina was the only one who'd choose me. And that might not be enough.

"You should ask Caelum to help," Marina said, like she was reading my mind. "Help you get your powers back or at least figure out how to summon them again."

"Caelum?" I repeated. He did seem nice—friendly, even.

"He's a demon, but he's walking around in a reincarnated human version of himself. He's good at suppressing and summoning his power when needed."

"Suppressing? You think *that's* what I'm doing?"

She nodded. "I think your body's been suppressing your energy for so long, you don't even know how to stop it."

"And Caelum's going to teach me how?"

"I just think he can," she shrugged.

It was worth a shot. "I guess I can talk to him."

"You want me to ask?"

"No. I think I can handle it. He and Soren aren't that hard to talk to."

Marina laughed. "Yeah, they're both teddy bears."

I hoped so. Teddy bears who might kill me to save their best friend.

"What are we doing today?" I asked.

"Looks like more research."

"Are we helping?" I asked. "I don't know how to translate those old-ass books. Plus they smell awful."

Marina laughed. "No, we'd just be a distraction. I want you to spend the day training and meditating, trying to summon your power."

"So I should—"

"Go talk to Caelum!"

"Right, right." I pushed up from the bed.

"Wait!" she tossed me a shirt. "You can't go to the third floor in just your bra. All the boys are up there."

"Oh crap!" I quickly pulled the shirt over my head and rushed out. I took the grimy old stairwell—it was faster than the prehistoric elevator. I reached the third floor and froze.

I forgot to ask which room was his.

I started to head back when the elevator dinged. I turned to see who stepped out.

It was Jude. Holding a pile of snacks and a soda.

"Hey, Jude," I said.

He looked annoyed.

"I was looking for Caelum. I don't know his room number."

Jude rolled his eyes and walked past me. "Sorry, can't help you."

"What? Why?"

He pulled out his keycard and opened a door—Soren was standing there on the other side, about to open it himself.

"Did you get the snacks?" Soren asked. "Wait—why is there only one soda?"

"You didn't say you wanted one. Go get it yourself. I'm not your servant," Jude snapped.

"Man, last time I let *you* go do our snack run."

"I didn't want to go!"

"Fair is fair. Besides, not my fault you lost rock-paper-scissors!"

I laughed. They both turned to me.

"Oh, hey Maeve," Soren said. "What's up?"

"Not much. Just trying to find Caelum's room."

"He's down that way in 309. And Asshole—I mean, Ryu—is in 307."

I laughed. "Thanks, Soren."

"No problem. Hey, we've got snacks if you wanna come in."

"No!" Jude barked. "Don't invite her in here."

"What? Why not?" Soren whispered.

"Because I don't want to hang out with her," Jude hissed back.

"That's okay," I said before they could argue more. "I'm just looking for Caelum. I'm going to train today, Jude. While everyone's researching. I'm trying hard to figure out how to draw out my powers. That way, you can stop calling me useless."

He was silent for a moment. Then that cocky smirk crossed his face. "Well, it's about time. Good luck with that."

I gave him a fake smile. Then a real one for Soren. "Bye, Soren."

"See ya later, Maeve!" Soren called as Jude slammed the door behind him.

I walked to room 309, straightened my clothes, flipped my hair back, and knocked.

No answer.

I knocked again. Still nothing.

Then the door opened in front of me.

Big maroon eyes—just like Marina's—stared back at me just as confused as I was.

Ryu.

Crap! Soren must've mixed up the room numbers. I stood frozen in front of him like a total idiot.

Without even saying a word, the guy had *what do you want* written all over his face.

I smiled awkwardly, backing away from the door a bit. "Oh—Ryu! I'm sorry, I was looking for Caelum. But clearly, he's not here and you are definitely not him. I've got the wrong room. So sorry to bother you."

Without saying a word, he stepped out and pointed silently toward 307.

"Right. Got it. Thanks," I mumbled.

He backed into his room and shut the door.

Why was he like this?

I knocked on Caelum's door. No answer.

He must be upstairs with Auri and Gwen doing research. Made sense—he used to be a demon and was supposedly a thousand years old according to Marina. He is way older than her and Ryu. He might understand the old texts without translation.

I guess I'd leave the boys alone. I'd go meditate by myself—see what I could figure out. The beach seemed like a good place. The weather was kind of gloomy, but quiet. No one else out there. Not even the ghost since it was daylight.

I needed to be helpful. I needed to be useful. Not just for the team—but to protect myself.

Chapter Twenty-Three
Jude

"Give it back, you—!" I shouted.

"NO!" Soren shouted back, pushing my face with one hand as I lunged forward. He had the chocolate bar in the other. "You already get to keep the soda! It's only fair I get to eat the 'chocolatey choc-tee-tee nut bar!'"

"No, that's my chocolate, dumbass. I bought it!" I swung a punch, but missed. He was quicker than usual.

"I gave you money!" he argued, still struggling with me.

"Yeah, for the rest of the snacks! *This* chocolate is mine!"

"Why didn't you get two, you selfish dick?!"

"Because I ran out of coins! Give me the goddamn chocolate!"

"Go to hell!"

We kept struggling while he tried to open the wrapper with one hand.

"You wouldn't dare! One bite and I'm going to kill you—"

And just like that, he did it. Dropped the whole damn chocolate bar into his mouth.

He either let go of my arm or I broke free—honestly, not sure which. I was too busy being mentally destroyed after seeing him slobber all over *my* nut bar.

"I hate you," I said, giving him a death glare. "You could've at least broken it in half."

"Hmm... so tasty!" he said through a mouthful. "This is what you get for not sharing those chips the other night."

"That was different!"

"How?" he snapped.

Just then, I heard a buzzing sound from my bed under the covers. I walked over, flipping through the sheets until I found my phone. Kayo was calling.

"Hey baby," I answered, walking out to the balcony to escape the chocolate thief's nonsense.

"Jude is everything okay?" she asked, calm but clearly concerned.

I slid the balcony door shut. "Everything is... well, a little up in the air."

"What's that supposed to mean?"

I hadn't told her the full truth yet. Not about the seal. Not about how one of us has to possibly bleed out. What was the point of making her worry when she couldn't even do anything from the other side of the world?

"Jude. Tell me the truth."

"I don't know how."

"It's Daisy, isn't it? Or Maeve?"

"She goes by Maeve. That's her first name," I

corrected lazily, dropping into a chair, phone in one hand, head down in the other.

"Jude. Just tell me."

"It's just... Kayo, there's a very difficult choice. A decision I can't—"

"I knew this was going to happen," she cut me off.

"Huh?"

"I knew it. I pretty much called it before you left," she said, voice sharp. Angry.

"What are you even talking about?" I asked, feeling defensive.

"A choice, right? You and Maeve?"

"Yeah?" I said, starting to wonder if Soren had told her something about the seal already.

"I see."

"More like or *Maeve*," I corrected her, debating whether to explain the full situation.

"Well, let me make the choice easier for you," she said. "I'm done. Maeve can have you. You're so conflicted. Right? Go be with her if that's what you want so bad."

"Wait, what? Kayo—"

"No, Jude. I have to go. There's really not a lot left to say. I wish you and that super skank the best of—"

"KAYO," I snapped. "I'M NOT CHOOSING HER! I DON'T EVEN LIKE HER!"

There was nothing but silence. I didn't even know if she was still on the phone.

"Hello?"

"...Then what are you saying? What choice do you have?"

I sighed. Then I told her everything. About the portal. About King Aurelius screwing us over. The Spirit World not really helping. The seal. The blood. Everything.

She was quiet for a moment. Then, "Wow. Jude, I—I feel terrible. I'm so sorry. I'm coming there. I'll get a flight and then take a bus the rest of the way to Starbrook. I can maybe be there by tomorrow."

"No," I said. "It's way too dangerous. I already have enough to worry about."

That was the truth. I had to keep myself alive. And Maeve, whose powers were currently in factory-reset mode. Adding Kayo to the list? No thanks.

"I feel so useless," she said, crying.

"I know," I said. "That's why I didn't tell you."

"I'm glad you did."

"You always know when I'm hiding something. You know me too well."

"That I do. And I thought for sure you met Maeve and you two *bonded* over the mission and the fact that you're both Veil—"

"Kayo. Please stop. Please. I don't like her. She's— I just don't. Not even a little."

"I'm more worried about you dying now."

"Yeah. Same here. That's what I'm trying to avoid."

We both went quiet again. I could hear the waves in the background. I looked down at the beach and saw Ryu walking. Probably heading off to train.

"I need to go," I told her. "I should go train with the guys."

"Of course," she said softly.

Then, just as I was about to say goodbye—

"Um, Jude," she said.

"Hmm?"

"If it comes down to it... you or Maeve. If the combo blood plan doesn't work..., what will you do?"

She was really asking if I'd kill Maeve to save myself.

And trust me—I'd thought about it. But that would make me exactly what King Aurelius wanted. And I'm not a puppet. I couldn't do it. I wouldn't kill another Veil-keeper, even if it meant dying.

"I don't know," I said honestly. "I guess... whichever one of us bleeds out first. But I'm not going to hurt her."

"Oh," Kayo said. "You wouldn't be the man I love if you did. But... I still hope you do what it takes to come back to me. Is that selfish?"

I exhaled hard. Of course I'd thought about it. But no—I wouldn't.

"I'll let you go," she said. "Call me later, okay? I need to hear from you now that I know all this."

"Yeah. I will. I promise. I love you."

"I love you too."

The call ended. I stared at my phone for a moment before sliding it into my pocket.

I walked to the balcony. Looked down.

I could totally make that jump.

"HEY RYU!" I yelled, waving my arms.

He turned, hands in his pockets. No expression. Typical.

"WAIT UP! I'M COMING DOWN!" I shouted.

Then I climbed the railing and jumped off the third-floor balcony.

I landed solid. Nice. Still had it.

(*Kids, don't try that at home. I have superpowers. You don't.*)

I took off running across the patio and onto the beach. The sand gave my legs a little extra workout. Ryu was still standing, waiting. Calm. Like always.

"Hey man, you going to train?"

He nodded.

"Cool. Let's go."

He was headed toward the forest, clearly. He wasn't the type to just sit around and wait. And I was down for that. Plus, training with Ryu was way different than going in there with Maeve. We walked together, the humidity thick and the waves behind us crashing harder. A storm was coming. We'd be back before it hit.

Unless we ran into another creepy skin walker demon.

Ryu had his daggers strapped to his back. He did the sickest techniques with those things. Not only could he make them ignite with fire, but he moved so fast his enemies didn't even realize they'd been sliced to ribbons.

Ryu was cutthroat. Lethal. I'd seen him get stronger over the years, and all I could think as we disappeared into the trees was: I'm just glad he's on *our* side.

Chapter Twenty-Four
Marina

Maeve and I went to the small diner again, across the street from the inn. We listened as the static-filled radio droned on about another incoming storm—how they'd been worse lately, more unpredictable than ever. It's true. It's been storming back-to-back the past two days.

"Might have something to do with the portal," Maeve said, sipping her hot coffee. "Auri says the extra demonic energy in the area can't be helping matters."

"Aren't you going to eat something with that?" I asked, eyeing the emerald, green mug she held to her face. "You know coffee gives you the jitters."

"I'm not really hungry right now," she said, setting the mug down. "Eating and sleeping's gotten harder. This place, this mission, not knowing what to even expect... I just feel so—"

"Helpless?" I offered.

"That, and maybe a little... hopeless. I feel like there's no point in trying if—"

"We have a plan," I interrupted gently. "And we're meeting with the others after this. It's been a couple of days—maybe they've come up with something better."

She blinked and looked around the diner, taking another big sip of her coffee. She stared into the mug like it held the answers to the universe.

"Come on," I said, standing up. "Finish that so we can get to the meeting. We don't want to be the reason they're held up."

"Right," she agreed taking a big swig.

We pushed our chairs back at the same time and headed to the counter to pay.

"How was it?" the woman behind the counter asked.

"Fine," Maeve answered.

A little too vague. I didn't want the woman to feel offended.

"It was great, thank you," I added, handing over the card.

She gave me the receipt. I scribbled my name and thanked her again before we stepped outside.

The wind had picked up, blowing hard enough to whip our hair in every direction. We jogged across the empty street and back to the inn.

Inside, the front desk guy—sat at his usual post. He nodded as we passed. He sits in that chair every single day. How was he not bored?

I pressed the button for the elevator. Maeve started pulling out her hair again.

"Stop," I whispered.

She caught herself and dropped her hands.

The elevator finally opened.

"Shall we?" I said.

She didn't answer, just stepped in.

Every time we had a meeting, Maeve left overthinking every interaction. This one would be no different.

We reached the top floor and headed straight to Aurelius's room. The door was cracked open again.

Inside, only Ryu and Jude were there.

"Where is everyone?" I asked. "Soren's not here?"

"Soren said he had a stomachache," Jude replied. "Stayed in his room. Told me to fill him in later."

I nodded. "Oh."

The room was dead quiet. Not surprising with my brother there, but even Jude sat sprawled on the couch, arms stretched, feet on the coffee table. Ryu leaned against the arm of the couch like usual.

Maeve sat across from Jude. I took the spot between her and my brother. No one looked at each other. The tension in the room was thick.

There was an old wall clock ticking. I'd never noticed it before. It was so quiet now, I couldn't *not* notice. I focused on my breathing, afraid it was too loud.

Jude adjusted in his seat, leaned forward, rubbed his face, and said, "Maeve, you should go home."

We all looked at him—except Ryu, who already looked bored before the conversation even started.

I was about to say something, but Maeve spoke first.

"I would if I could," she replied. "I'm not as thrilled to be here as you seem to think."

"You *can* go," Jude said. "Ryu and I went back into the woods the other day. Found five more of those demons lurking around. They were stronger. If you're struggling with just one, you're no use to us here. You'll just get in the way. I mean—you already are."

I could tell she was offended. Her hands balled into fists on her lap.

"Jude," she said calmly. "I'm going to say this in the nicest way possible..."

He looked up at her.

"I would *really* appreciate it if you could shut the fuck up."

That was the nicest way?

Even Ryu glanced over. I braced myself for Jude's response. The Jude I remembered wouldn't let that slide —and I was right.

"So that's how you talk to the person— the *only* person here saving your ass," he snapped. "No one is going to carry your dead weight. You're a damn Veilkeeper, and you act shocked you were even summoned here for this mission. Get a grip, Princess. That whole 'I'm going to go train' crap? How dumb can you be? You should've been training *years* ago. Not the day before we might have to fight! That's like doing your homework five minutes before it's due!"

Maeve crossed her arms. Her eyes looked glassy, but she wasn't crying yet.

"You don't even know what the hell you're talking about," she muttered.

"Oh no, I *do*," Jude shot back. "You're used to people fighting your battles. Used to be the guys in America, now it's me. Like, 'Oh, I don't need to train—the other Veilkeeper can handle it all while I live my glamorous superstar life.'"

"That's not even tr—"

He kept going. It was like he'd been bottling it all up and finally let it pour.

"It *is* true. And the problem I have, Maeve, is that your unwillingness to be prepared is putting *my* life at stake—and the whole damn planet. We took an oath to protect this world. You remember that? When you were called as a kid? The only way out of the Spirit World was agreeing to serve as a Veilkeeper. That oath doesn't just disappear because you want to be a singer or whatever. You're a *keeper*. First and always! I don't like you because I find you disrespectful. Not just to me, but to Kosei— who, by the way, risked his life for all of us. And now you act like training is optional? Like we should just have your back while you don't have ours?"

"Jude," I said, trying to cut in. "It's not Maeve's fault."

"I know you want to protect her, Marina. Mean ole Jude talking down to Princess Daisy, right? But there's a difference in defending someone and *enabling* them."

I could feel Ryu glance at me. My cheeks were hot.

"Oh, so now I'm enabling her?" I snapped. "To what —get herself killed? Explain that to me, Jude."

"You making excuses for why she's weak isn't helping."

"I'm not making excuses!"

"But you are!" he raised his voice to match mine. I

could hear the frustration. Maeve sat there, fists clenched, shrinking.

Then the door opened. Not Auri and Gwen. Just Soren.

Tension eased slightly.

"Hey, guys. I could hear Jude yelling from the hall. What's going on?" he asked.

"It's nothing," Jude muttered. "Where've you been? Thought you said you were sick."

"Oh, uh—I feel better now. Crisis averted."

"Uh huh," Jude said. "What'd you do, blow up the shitter again?"

Soren's face turned red. "Jude, you *jerkface*! Shut up! You don't have to say that in front of Marina!"

"Yeah, yeah. Everyone wants me to shut up. Fine. I won't say another word."

And he didn't. Thankfully.

Maeve kept staring at her hands, knuckles white. Her eyes were even glossier now. She was furious—and holding it in. Jude could tell too. He sat back, cocky, watching her like he *wanted* this reaction.

Whether he meant everything he said or just wanted to provoke her, I couldn't tell. Maybe it was both.

But here we were—supposed to be united in the face of catastrophe, and we couldn't even get along.

The wind howled outside. We all stared out the window, watching the chaotic storm unfold on the beach.

I wondered how much longer Auri and Gwen would be. Maeve wasn't going to last much longer like this. I knew it. Her anger would turn to tears, and I couldn't let Jude get the satisfaction of seeing her fall apart.

Then Caelum entered the room.

"Auri and Gwen are on their way," he said. "They had to file a report with Spirit World."

He looked around, scanning the room. You could tell he felt the tension immediately.

He turned to me, raising an eyebrow. "What did I miss?"

Chapter Twenty-Five
Aurelius

I arrived at the meeting, regrettably late. Gwen and I had just finished sending our report to the Spirit World—something we were required to do to keep my father in the loop. As we left the front desk, we caught the local news playing on the lobby television, courtesy of the front desk manager. I say "manager," but I'm pretty sure he's the only one working at the inn.

That's when we saw it—a missing persons report. A man named Travis Goins. I took in the details briefly, then headed upstairs to meet with the others. Gwen followed behind me as always.

When I stepped into the room, no one said a word. The whole team looked tired and on edge. I immediately sensed I had missed something—but I had more pressing matters to address.

"I'm sorry, everyone. We're running a bit behind today," I said, walking toward the end of the couches, where I usually stood during our briefings. Everyone else either sat on or leaned against the furniture. Gwen stood slightly off to the side, focused on the tablet in her hands.

She walked over and handed it to me just as I removed my light cloak and laid it over the back of a chair.

"This man," I said, holding up the tablet so everyone could see, "his name is Travis Goins. He's missing."

"Okay?" Jude said, arms crossed and unimpressed. "Pretty obvious what happened. He's demon food."

Everyone looked at him.

"Remember when Maeve and I went into the woods a few days ago?" he continued.

"Yes, I recall you not following instructions. Go on," I said dryly.

"Well, the demon we saw was mid-feast before I rudely interrupted. I'm not sure if it was Travis, but it was definitely one of the missing townsfolk. Their fate's pretty clear."

I nodded. He wasn't wrong. Travis had likely been eaten.

"It couldn't have been—" Maeve spoke up.

Everyone turned to her.

"Oh, I just mean—I met him. Travis. He's the guy who wouldn't stop following me the night Caelum and Ryu arrived. It couldn't have been him that Jude and I found in the woods."

Then she shrank into herself on the couch. This wasn't the Maeve I used to know. She wasn't the same confident young girl who once sat in meetings with Orpheus and me, offering ideas and speaking up with boldness. This version of Maeve was hesitant— shrinking in front of everyone. It made me wonder what exactly I had missed before walking in. What had been said in this room?

Jude nodded, dismissive. "Okay, like I said—who cares?"

"Damn, man. Really?" Soren shot back.

"What?" Jude shrugged. "We know he's dead. Let's move on and figure out how to stop this before more people die. That's all I'm saying."

I didn't argue with Jude—yet. I turned back to Maeve, who hesitated before continuing.

"He ran off toward the beach the last time I saw him. What if—" She stopped. Her eyes flicked to Jude, and then she shut down again. I saw it clearly—he was intimidating her. Baiting her, maybe even trying to provoke her powers into awakening. It wouldn't surprise me if this was all part of some method behind his madness. But it was backfiring. She wasn't lashing out—she was shutting down.

"Maeve?" Gwen prompted gently.

"What if the demons didn't kill him?" she said.

Jude scoffed. "Yeah, okay Maeve."

Gwen and I both gave him a sharp look. He didn't flinch.

Maeve looked around, anxiety radiating off her as the room fell quiet again.

"I just mean—what if he went down to the beach? It was night. What if... it was Gladys?"

The room was silent again. Everyone looked confused. I saw Ryu glance up, cock a brow, then look down again. Caelum watched Maeve with an open expression, waiting to hear more. Soren looked like his mind was elsewhere. Marina gave Maeve a sympathetic look, lips pursed together tightly.

And then Jude: "Who the fuck is Gladys?" He raised his voice, owning the space and making her feel even smaller.

Maeve didn't answer.

Soren stepped in. "Gladys is a ghost—or at least Maeve thinks she saw one on the beach."

He was trying to be supportive, even if he didn't entirely believe it. I couldn't say I did either.

"It was just an idea," Maeve said, voice small, eyes on her hands.

"Yeah, a useless one—as usual," Jude muttered with a laugh.

I was going to have to address his behavior. He was clearly stressed, but bullying his teammate was unacceptable.

"Like I said," Maeve said with more bite, "just an idea. You don't have to keep being a jerk."

"Hey, I've got an idea," Jude replied. "Why don't Maeve and Marina just go home?"

Here we go again.

Before I could speak, Soren jumped in.

"Jude, everyone is getting tired of your shit, man. Maeve may not have done much yet, but you sure as hell aren't helping with your constant crap."

Jude scoffed, arms crossed, sitting back like none of this applied to him.

"We're a team," Soren continued, "and the girls are part of it. Just because Kayo's got you on a tight leash doesn't mean you need to be a dickhead to every other woman."

He turned to Maeve. "I'm glad you're here. I'm sure your powers will come back any day now. And even if they don't, we've got your back. Even if *ass-face* over there doesn't."

Maeve gave him a small smile, her shoulders relaxing just a little.

"Thank you," she said quietly.

Jude scoffed again.

Soren looked at me, giving me the floor.

"Jude, we'll talk after this meeting," I said firmly.

"Why wait?" he challenged. "Let's just get the lecture over with now."

I exhaled. "You know Maeve leaving isn't an option. The Spirit World—and my father—would forbid it. Whether you want to admit it or not, the two of you need each other."

Jude didn't respond. He just shook his head and rolled his eyes, spiraling under the pressure.

I couldn't blame him for cracking. But I needed him to pull it together, because what I was about to say wasn't going to be easy for anyone.

I walked to the sliding glass doors. The storm outside was getting worse— wind howling, waves crashing.

"It's time," I said, turning back to the group. "No more fighting each other. Because after this storm passes, we're splitting into teams."

Everyone stared at me.

"We're going to locate the portal," I continued, "and perform the ritual to seal it."

Dead silence.

Even Jude looked nervous—though he tried to hide it.

I saw Maeve glance at Marina. Marina placed a hand on her arm protectively, her red eyes locked on me like a warning. I knew this wasn't what the group wanted to hear, not after whatever just went down before I arrived. But we had no choice.

Too many people had died already.

If we didn't act soon, it would only get worse—more deaths, more demons, more storms.

The portal had to be closed.

And it had to be closed now.

Chapter Twenty-Six
Maeve

In the hallway after the meeting, Caelum approached me. I thought he was going to comment on all the drama that had just gone down—even though he missed half of it.

"Heard you were looking for me the other day," he said with a warm smile.

He was beautiful up close—almost unreal. His naturally bright cherry red hair was long down his back, and his eyes were a pretty gray color. If this was his human form, I couldn't even imagine what he looked like as a demon.

"Oh, yes," I said, suddenly nervous. His beauty was... a little intimidating. "I was, but I figured you were probably really busy."

"Nonsense," he said smoothly. "What's up?"

Just as I was about to answer, Ryu and Marina walked out of Auri's room. Marina stopped next to me. Ryu kept walking toward the stairs, not even looking at me—like I didn't exist.

Caelum must've noticed the shift in my expression.

"Don't worry," he said, eyes closing for a moment but smile still warm. "You're not imagining things. It's nothing personal. He's like that with everyone."

"I tried to tell her that," Marina laughed.

"It's true. Both of us would know," Caelum added.

"All too well," Marina agreed. "I'm heading back to the room. Maeve—don't go outside."

"I know," I replied. She sounded more like *my* sister than Ryu's sometimes. "I'll be there soon."

She walked off toward the stairs. We'd learned by now that they were faster than the ancient elevator.

After she left, I looked back and saw Caelum's gaze still on me, waiting patiently for me to say why I'd wanted to talk to him in the first place.

"Oh, right," I said. "I've been having trouble... trying to access my powers. Marina thinks I might be unintentionally suppressing them."

He nodded slightly, like he was waiting for more. That was all I had to say, but I kept rambling anyway.

"I was wondering if maybe... if you had time, you could help me figure out how to—I don't know the word."

"Awaken?" he offered. "Although that sounds like something out of a cheesy tv show."

I laughed. He was so down to earth for someone who looked so celestial. I tried not to seem flirty. At all.

"Sure," he said, "I can help wake up your powers."

"Wow, really?"

"Yeah. When do you want to start?" he asked, tilting his head.

His voice was so kind, almost like he was talking to a

kid. Then again, if Marina was right and he was over a thousand years old... maybe I was a kid to him.

"Now," I said quickly. "Uh—right now if you can."

"Alright," he smiled. "Let's hit that poor excuse of a workout room on the first floor. We'll make Jude eat his words."

He winked, turned, and headed toward the stairs.

I knew I was blushing. I prayed he wouldn't turn around and see my face. We entered the stairwell, and he jogged down ahead of me with long, elegant strides. I hurried to keep up.

We passed the lobby and went down a hallway I hadn't been in yet. There was a laundry room and, beside it, a sad little gym with mirrors, a few weights, two yoga mats and a giant purple bouncy ball in the corner.

"This is their gym?" I asked, laughing.

"Pathetic, right?" he grinned. "Honestly, I'm surprised we even have one at all."

I sat down on one of the two yoga mats already spread out. Cross-legged, straight-backed. He sat across from me the same way—just a foot away.

He gazed directly into my eyes, and I immediately felt my cheeks go hot. Not from tears like earlier during the meeting—but from the sheer intensity of his focus. He was so... dreamy.

Then he held out his right hand.

"Uh—" I said, taking it with my left. The moment our hands met, I felt a jolt. Not warm. Not comforting. It was electric. Shocking. I snatched my hand away.

"What was that for? That hurt! Why did you shock me?!" I snapped.

"That wasn't me," he said gently. "That was you."

I narrowed my eyes. Was he lying?

He held out his hand again. I hesitated. Was Caelum secretly evil? The beautiful ones usually are.

He caught the hesitation on my face.

"Don't worry," he said. "This time you'll be ready."

"No, I don't want to—" I scowled. "That wasn't very nice."

He shrugged. "Well, girl, maybe your power isn't very nice."

"My power?"

"Let's go again."

Reluctantly, I reached for his hand again—this time gripping tighter. He chuckled softly.

"Focus," he said.

The room went quiet. This time, at first, I felt nothing. I stared into his eyes, then—JOLT.

That same electric sensation. But it slowed. Became bearable. Like my body was adjusting.

I tried to pull away, but he held on. Firm.

"Hold on," he said calmly.

Then everything around me faded. The storm outside, the buzzing of the lights—all muted. Blue and white sparks shimmered between our hands. My eyes fluttered shut. I leaned into the feeling.

And then—I felt it. Something old. Something familiar.

My Veil Ki...

I opened my eyes. It looked like flames—or a mirage of flames—dancing faintly in the space between us. My breath caught. I looked at Caelum, who was still watching me closely.

Then—SLAM. The door swung open violently, no stopper to catch it.

The moment shattered. I jerked out of the daze like I'd just woken from a deep nap. I turned to see, the front desk guy, standing in the doorway.

His arms were crossed. "You kids aren't smoking in here, are you?"

Caelum and I looked at each other—our hands still connected.

"No," I said quickly.

"We're meditating," Caelum added politely.

He squinted. "Okay. No burning stuff. No incense. You might not know by looking at it, but this big, beautiful inn caught fire once. We don't want a repeat."

He gave us both a suspicious look before finally shutting the door.

"Well," Caelum said, "that explains a lot. Honestly, I'm starting to think they should've just let this place burn down and rebuilt it."

I laughed. But then I turned serious.

"What *was* that?" I asked. "That electric thing you did to me?"

"Me? I didn't do anything," he said. "That was all you."

"Huh?" I asked, eyes wide. Our fingers were still intertwined. I blushed again and quickly pulled my hand away.

"Let me explain," he said. "That jolt? That was your

power waking up. I didn't shock you. I did, however, hypnotize you."

"Hypnotize?" My eyes went wide again. "How?"

"Just a little trick I learned—long before you were born. Don't worry, I'm not in your head. I just nudged your body into a fight-or-flight state. You chose fight. And boom—your power surfaced. Quite some power you've got by the way. But everything you felt? That was *you*. I just poked the bear."

"You really think I'm strong?" I asked, uncertain.

"Maeve—yes," he said seriously. "Why don't you think you're powerful?"

"I don't know..."

"You're the same girl who defeated Ihadurca all those years ago. You've saved the Earth—and more than that, the entire universe."

"Oh." I looked away awkwardly. "So you heard?"

"Of course. We've all heard—me, Jude, Ryu."

He looked almost sad. "It's honestly a shame we're only meeting now. Especially under these circumstances."

"Yeah..." I glanced up at the small window as a roar of thunder made it rattle. The sky outside was darker now, the storm was getting worse. My stomach growled. I regretted not eating earlier because I definitely wasn't leaving the inn now to go get food.

"I felt my Veil Ki inside me," I said. "It was like—"

"A storm?" he offered glancing at the window.

"Yeah. How do I use it in battle, like Jude does? He used a moon energy blast the other day. How can I do something like that?"

He crossed his arms, thoughtful. "How did you do it before?"

"I don't remember," I admitted. "It's been years."

I thought harder. And then it hit me—every time I accessed my power, I'd been scared. Backed into a corner. I'd only tapped into it in life-or-death moments.

"I need to be scared," I said aloud.

He looked at me again with that intense gaze—God, he was handsome.

"But wait... I *was* scared the other day. That demon with Jude? My powers didn't show up."

"Maybe not scared enough," he said. "Maybe because Jude was there, some part of you knew you'd be okay."

"Maybe," I whispered, disappointed.

"Hey, don't worry. The power's there—we saw it. I felt it. Now that it's awake, it'll come through again."

"I hope you're right."

He stood up and offered his hand. I took it, letting him help me to my feet.

"Thanks."

"No problem," he said, still looking at me. "We'll figure this out. Let's go. Marina's probably wondering where you are."

He winked again.

Oh boy. He was *something else.* I didn't know what to think of him—but I was grateful. For his help. For his kindness. For his belief in me.

So, what if Jude and Ryu didn't like me?

I still had Auri and Gwen—working nonstop to save me. I had Marina, my rock. Soren, who stood up for me today. And now Caelum, who was helping me remember how powerful I used to be.

When walking back to my room—I felt somewhat hopeful.

Even if it was just for a few seconds.

Chapter Twenty-Seven
Soren

The storm had gotten worse. I almost wondered if we should've just retreated inland until it passed instead of staying right here on the ocean. Everyone in Starbrook was boarding up their windows earlier this morning, so they clearly knew it was going to be rough. And apparently, because of the spike in demonic activity, Aurelius said we should expect this one to be even more unpredictable than usual.

Great.

"At least tomorrow is going to be romantic," I said, laying on my back and resting the book I was reading on my chest.

"Yeah? And how's that?" Jude asked, walking around the room, still scrolling through his phone, holding it up like the higher angle would magically give him better reception.

"Aurelius said we'd be splitting into teams. It only makes sense that Marina and I pair up again."

"Uh-huh," Jude muttered, still distracted by his phone.

"You'll probably get paired with Maeve—you know, since the two of you might have to do a blood transfusion to close the seal."

I stared up at the ceiling, wondering how they'd even know when the seal had enough blood. Would the portal just close? Would there be fireworks? Or would some tiny demon guy pop out and say, "Wish granted" like this was some kind of cursed genie ritual?

"Yeah," Jude said, "so you're excited about tomorrow even though I might have to nearly bleed to death to save the world. But hey, at least Soren gets to sit next to Marina and stare at her like a creep for a few hours."

I had no comeback. "Shut up," was all I could say.

But he was right. I wasn't being very empathetic. I guess I figured if I joked about it, it wouldn't feel as real—like if I downplayed the situation in my head, it wouldn't weigh so heavily. But here I was, goofing off while Jude might really get hurt. Or worse.

"Hey, man," I sat up. "I'm sorry."

He waved a hand dismissively still pacing and scrolling.

Then—boom.

The lights cut off without warning. The low hum of electricity and buzzing from the walls vanished, leaving nothing but silence. I swung my legs over the side of the bed.

"Geez. I wonder how long it'll be like this," I said.

"Who knows," Jude replied.

Thunder rattled the whole building, and lightning cracked so violently I swore it hit right outside.

"This storm is not playing around."

"Storm? This feels more like a hurricane."

"What's the difference?" He asked.

"Gee someone didn't pay attention in science class. One of them is worse or whatever."

The air turned thick and humid. I was already sweating.

"Let's go downstairs and ask that desk guy about the backup generator," I said.

"What?"

"Remember? He told us about it—backups in case of a storm."

"No?"

"You never listen. Come on."

"Ugh," Jude groaned, dragging his feet. "Why don't you just go?"

"Because!"

"Don't tell me you're scared," he smirked, "Scared of the dark?"

"No. But you aren't doing anything. You can come with me."

"Scared ghost Gladys is gonna come out and get ya?" He lunged forward with his hands like claws.

"Just come on." I flinched a little.

I fumbled to the door, still adjusting to the darkness. Jude huffed but followed me. His grumbling echoed all the way down the stairs.

When we reached the lobby, something immediately felt bizarre.

"Jude?" I whispered.

"Yeah. I feel it too."

Then—

"PLEASE HELP ME!"

We sprinted toward the sound and found the front desk guy, swatting at one of those demon things. One of the tall, long-armed, sharp-toothed ones Jude had described before. This was my first time seeing it up close. And yeah—it was hideous.

"AHH! GET IT AWAY!" the man screamed, cowering as the thing shrieked with jaws stretched wide, gooey drool dripping down its fangs. The sound it made didn't sound earthly. It reminded me of what a dinosaur might have sounded like on that one movie.

"Get down!" Jude shouted, raising a hand and blasting the scary monster with his Veil Ki. The force was massive—blue and silver sparks launched the demon straight through the broken front doors.

The creature staggered up, snarling, then lunged back at Jude.

I rushed to desk guy while Jude went head-to-head with the thing. He'd fought a few of these things before, so I wasn't too worried. Still, the way they crashed around the lobby, knocking over furniture, was intense.

Desk guy's right arm was gashed up, bleeding badly. He had cuts all over—face, arms, everywhere.

"Ahh, it busted in through the door!" Desk guy said, shaking. "There were more of them!"

"More?" I asked—but then the demon came crashing back toward us, and I had to duck.

Jude grabbed it by the snout, powered up, and blasted it point-blank. It dropped, lifeless, right in front of us.

"What the hell was that thing?!" Desk guy gasped.

"You got a first aid kit?" Jude asked, out of breath.

"In the closet behind the desk," he said.

Jude darted to grab it. I noticed his hand was bleeding—deep gash from the demon's swipe.

He came back and knelt down. I helped him pour alcohol on the wound and wrap it tight.

"Damn, man, that's a lot of blood."

"Yeah. And just think—I'm supposed to lose even more than this soon," he said flatly.

Outside, the storm raged on. Wind whipped through the open front of the inn, sending debris flying. The whole place was a mess.

"There's more of them," Desk guy said, trembling. "Maybe four, five... six? I don't know."

Jude stood. "We'll take care of it."

Desk dude was shaking so hard he looked like a human phone on vibrate.

"We've never had anything like this. Fires, yeah, from idiots smoking—but monsters? This is crazy!"

"We need to warn the others," I told Jude.

He nodded.

"Hey man," Jude said, "you need to hide. Go in that closet and stay there."

"What?!" Desk guy's eyes bulged. "You want me to stay here?! While those things are out there?! No way!"

"It's the safest place," I told him.

"You think this place is safe?! This place is cursed!"

"Dude. Just get in the closet," Jude said, firmer now.

"No!" he shouted. He bolted past us, toward the shattered entrance. "I'm going home!"

"Don't!" I yelled. "There could be more demons out there!"

"I'm not dying here!"

And then—flash.

A blinding light struck the ground. We heard him scream just before it hit him. Lightning.

It lit up the whole lobby for a second, then vanished. When I blinked the light out of my eyes, I saw him—he laid there fried. Not moving.

"Well... he's dead," Jude said, hands on hips. "Good grief."

I stood frozen. I'd never seen anyone die like that before. "We tried to stop him," I muttered.

"It can't be helped now," Jude said. Then he turned, sprinting for the stairs. "Come on. We have to warn the others."

"Right!" I followed close behind.

The storm wasn't finished yet. And neither were the demons.

Chapter Twenty-Eight
Maeve

"Shh!" Marina said to me as we stood behind our door, listening out into the hallway. The aura felt eerie. Someone or something was out there.

It was in that moment it hit me. I had to protect Marina. I had relied so heavily on my team, and lately on Jude, but something was coming for us. I was the only one that could stop it right now. I didn't know if the others were aware. Marina tried to call them, but no one was answering. And Ryu didn't even have a phone.

If I could get to the third floor, the boys will help me, I thought to myself. I wanted to find Caelum especially, since he's the only one here that was able to help draw out any bit of my power. I needed him like a crutch in this moment.

Just then I heard it. The sound. The same sound of the demon Jude and I met out in the woods the other day. It was here. Marina's eyes widened as she heard it too. I became stiff. What was I going to do? It sounded like there was more than just one. I froze in fear as my heart and mind started racing.

I have to do something.

"I have to go out there," I told Marina in a loud whisper. I started to stand, but she immediately pulled me back down.

"No, you can't, are you crazy?" she said, still holding onto my arm. "We have to wait for the guys. Surely, they sense that they're here."

"No," I shook my head. "I need to help. Do my part."

"Maeve, will you stop and think for a second! Your powers aren't even fully back!"

"I don't care. Maybe I can lead the demons upstairs away from you, and the boys will come out of their rooms to help me."

"That is the stupidest plan," she hissed, "we are fine keeping our asses right here!"

"But what if—" I was cut off by a huge slamming sound coming from the hall and those creatures screaming out. It sounded like they bashed in a door to another room.

"See!" I said to Marina, "they are going to try to come in here regardless, and then we'll be cornered."

"I still think it's best we just wait," she said. I listened again. They were slamming around screaming out something, almost like they were communicating in their weird demon language.

"No," I said.

"Maeve!"

"I have to go." I grabbed her head, kissed her forehead

hard, and then took off out the door. "Stay here!" I shouted back to her.

I couldn't hear what she was saying as I ran out of the room, my adrenaline was rushing. I was now in the hall. Door closed behind me, legs shaking, but I had to be brave. I looked down each side of the hallway. I didn't see anything, but I still heard them. It was coming from one of the rooms they'd busted the door into. I knew they would come back out here into the hall sooner or later.

I started walking slow toward the room I heard them screeching in. Their sounds getting louder and louder as I paced my slow steps down toward them. *I am walking toward my death.*

Just then I heard them—it sounded like they were coming out of the room they were in. I could hear them getting closer to the hall. I swallowed hard and froze in place.

Marina, I love you, I thought and closed my eyes tightly as I awaited them coming through the door. But then I felt something tug at my sleeve, grabbing my arm—gentle but with force at the same time. It pulled me around the corner of the hall, out of sight from the demons. I looked over to see who pulled me and who I just bumped into. A figure dressed in all black behind me. I turned to see pale white skin and big familiar red eyes—it was Ryu.

I gasped in shock, but his timing was impeccable. He signaled me to be quiet, putting his index finger to his mouth. He stood from his crouch and walked in front of me, pulling out two daggers from his back straps.

I watched as I could feel heat radiating off of him.

His demon energy—and then, before I could say anything, he stepped around the corner and the lanky white demon charged right at him with force.

"Ryu!" I shouted. But it was unnecessary.

Ryu moved so fast I could barely even see him. It was like flashes of light. He effortlessly dodged the demon, turning a flip in the air with his daggers and slicing through the demon as the blades of his daggers seemed to burn hot like they were in flames. He killed that thing much faster and easier than Jude did. *Holy shit*, I thought, watching him kill that demon easily and without any struggle. I was so impressed.

I couldn't watch for long because then three more of those ugly monstrous creatures came charging at us both. I don't know if it was just the situation we were in, where these things were running straight for us, but they seemed a lot bigger than the others. Two went straight for Ryu as he started to fight them off, and the other—well, you guessed it—teeth out and everything, straight toward little ole me.

"AH! FUCK!" I yelled as it tackled me, slamming me to the floor. Hitting my head. I could hear a ringing sound. A weird distant one, and I could hear—this is random—laughter, like it was from a distant memory of long ago. Maybe like the summers I spent at my grandmother's, when we were all outside playing with my cousins. I heard someone shouting, *"Maeve! Come inside!"* I heard that in the few seconds I was trying to recover from my head being slammed into the ground. I was somewhere else entirely. It dawned on me that my life might be starting to flash before my eyes. I might be dying.

The voice I was hearing turned manly. It wasn't my grandmother. It was a guy. "MAEVE! I'M COMING! HOLD ON!" I heard. It was coming from down the hall. I recognized it—it was Jude. I came to, and the first thing I saw was the demon standing over me, teeth out and coming right for me. I lifted my hand to its face. Everything happened so fast—and just like that, I blasted full force, my Veil Ki. An intense, full amount of it all at once. Like it had been backed up in supply. It was the same energy as what I conjured up with Caelum in practice, but this was it. My power lighting up the whole hallway, destroying and vaporizing the demon right before me to nothing.

I did it. I killed it. My power was back.

I sat up, hair I'm sure messy.

Jude ran toward me with what I couldn't believe—a huge smile on his face. He offered his hand to help me stand. I took it.

"Maeve! You did it! Your power—It was incredible!" he said with excitement and in as much disbelief as I was. My hand was still burning from that energy release. I laughed nervously, still shaken up. I looked over to see Ryu putting his daggers away on his back and the other two demons that attacked him dead on the floor.

Soren was standing next to Jude, surveying the area, then turning to me. "I don't sense anymore. Are you hurt?" he asked caringly.

I shook my head, "Nuh uh. I'm fine." I said, my whole

body feeling a huge rush and a wave of relief at the same time.

The lights somehow kicked back on. I sighed heavily and leaned into the wall.

"Maeve, you were incredible!" Jude continued in a tone of voice I had never heard before—it was actually friendly. "You blew that demon's face off."

"Yeah, that was hardcore," Soren added.

"Oh that? That was nothing." I joked.

Both Soren and Jude laughed.

"Right," Jude went along with me.

I sighed again, still shaking a little but trying to look tough in front of the guys.

Ryu stood with us, hands in his pockets, acting like nothing happened.

I stepped forward, still holding my hand as it still burned a little from releasing that energy blast. "Thank you, Ryu. You saved me."

He said—you guessed it! — NOTHING. He just looked away.

No "you're welcome." No "no problem." No "fuck you." Not a peep.

Oh well, I thought.

I heard a door slam. We looked around the corner to see Caelum coming from the stairwell down the hall.

We all ran toward him as well.

"Caelum! You missed it!" Jude said, still in the best mood I have ever seen him in. He was so fired up, hyping me up in front of everyone. "Maeve freaking destroyed that demon all by herself."

Caelum glanced over at the disgusting remains.

"Really? Well, I'm not too surprised," he said with a smile and another wink right at me. My cheeks flushed. I wish he would stop doing that. Sort of. Kind of. Not really.

I glanced over to see Ryu looking at me. But he looked away when I noticed. He definitely saw me smitten over his friend.

"I found the backup generator, but right when I started to mess with it, the lights came back on, so..." Caelum shrugged, looking over at me, still smiling. "I am just so proud of you."

"Yeah, really. Me too," Jude said, hitting my back.

I felt so included—with the exception of Ryu. But then I thought about what Marina said about not taking it personally, and that's just how he is. Then I remembered.

"Marina!" I said, running down the hall toward our room. Our door was open—which only made my heart race more. I ran inside to find her, Gwen, Auri—all together. She was okay.

I sighed in relief and walked over to her, falling into her arms. The boys had followed and were all behind us.

"Good work," Auri said.

"Caelum, Ryu—those demons, did either of you recognize them?" Gwen asked.

Ryu shook his head.

Caelum spoke. "No. I have never seen them. In all of my years in the world of apparitions, not once have I encountered them. The portal must be connected to a part of the demon world so tucked away, so remote...however I just can't imagine that creatures like those stay in one place. They seem very busy. I took out two of them downstairs when I went looking for the generator."

"Yeah, I'll say," Jude said.

"Well, whatever they are, at least we know how to kill them," Soren said.

"Says you," Jude said. "You haven't even killed one. Maeve's even got one up on you."

"Maeve?" Auri said in surprise, he, Gwen, and Marina all looking at me.

"You got your power back?" Marina said, squeezing me tighter in a side hug.

"Yeah," I said.

"This is wonderful news," Auri said. He started walking out of the room into the hallway.

We all followed.

He walked down to where the corpses of the demons lay on the floor, the ones Ryu killed. The one I killed—there was nothing left of.

"What a mess," he said. "These things weren't just here by random. They had to have been sent here by someone looking for us."

"Those were my thoughts too," Caelum agreed.

Auri held out his hand over the corpses and, with his spirit energy, made them completely vanish with a gold light—clearing them out like they were never here.

Wish he could have done that when they were alive, I thought.

"Someone knows we're here. My guess—the person or thing responsible for opening the portal," Jude said, crossing his arms. Face returning to the same serious expression I was used to.

"It just bugs me," he continued, "how is it that no one has any information on these demons or knows what part of the demon world they're from? Surely these big giant white fuckers stick out like sore thumbs even there."

"Maybe they're not from demon world," an unfamiliar voice spoke.

I jumped and turned, heart racing. It was—I couldn't believe it.

We all turned.

Ryu. He talked!

He stepped forward, hands in his pockets, still looking at Aurelius.

"I considered that too, Ryu," Aurelius said. "I just didn't know if that is better or worse."

"If not demon world, then where?" Marina asked.

"A different dimension, maybe," Auri shrugged. "Who's to say. There is still much to consider here."

They were all thinking about that, while I was still processing just hearing Ryu's voice for the first time. It was so different than how I imagined it sounding. I was trying not to say anything but—holy smokes. His voice was so— *hot*. I have never heard anyone sound like that!

And it was rare, since he hardly ever spoke.

We looked out the window to hear a commotion outside. It wasn't the storm—no, it had calmed down. It was other townsfolk, all over what appeared to be the front desk man, laying on the ground in front of the inn.

"Oh, don't worry. He's not dead," Auri said, as all of us watched them trying to lift him up to get him some help.

"What?" Soren asked. "How?"

"Wait, what happened?" I asked. "Was it the demon that did that to him?"

"No," Auri said. "That was something else. Completely random."

I was confused but let it go. He looked like he was going to be okay. I watched as the townsfolk were out there, continuing to help him and assessing the damage done to the front of the inn.

"We've got work to do," Auri said. "Gwen, Ryu, and Caelum—come to my room. The rest of you, good work. Go and rest for now. You're going to need it. Tomorrow we're heading out and will be exploring the hotspots in the woods. I need you all to be ready for whatever's to come."

I nodded. Marina tugged on my sleeve lightly and I followed her down the hall, waving at the rest of the team.

I was curious why Auri only wanted Caelum and Ryu upstairs to talk to him, but I was too tired to care enough to question it out loud.

Today had been eventful enough. Tomorrow might be worse.

Auri was right.

I needed to recharge.

I needed to finally try to get some sleep.

Chapter Twenty-Nine
Marina

Maeve told me the story right before she fell asleep. About how she defeated the demon using her energy blast, but right before that, she hit her head and had a nostalgic flashback of her childhood. It sounded to both of us like the setting was most likely her recalling the summers at her grandmother's house from her younger years—way before she was a famous singer or even a Veil-keeper. Just a young girl with a winding, twisted road ahead of her.

I'm not sure what was more traumatic for her: remembering those carefree, easy days or the monster showing her all his teeth right before it attempted to eat her alive. She started to talk about her brother Troy, and her cousins, then eventually a hard subject—her sweet, loving grandmother, whom I knew she missed dearly.

She talked, laughed, and remembered right up until she fell asleep last night. I went over to tuck her in better while she slept, and I noticed a single dried tear under her eyelid. She wasn't ready for what tomorrow would bring, but she figured she wouldn't suffer twice by staying up and worrying about what was to come. It was going to happen regardless.

As we walked downstairs to meet up with the team—after I forced her to eat a small breakfast in the form of yet another granola bar and protein shake (it was all I could get her to eat that morning since her nerves were already eating her alive)—I remained silent and deep in thought. We talked, but my mind was mainly focused on trying to figure out what the plan was for the day. *What did Aurelius have in store for Maeve?*

The storm had finally settled, and the weather was calm again. Somewhat gloomy, with the sun attempting to peek through—and of course, the reliable humidity we had all grown to expect.

We all met outside the inn. The front door still busted wide open, and we were all trying to watch our steps to avoid any glass the other townsfolk missed when they came to clean and attempt to help with removing anything hazardous.

I wondered how the inn keeper was doing and if anyone else was going to come run the front desk at the inn while he was in the hospital. So far, no one was there.

When we approached the group, everyone was already there. Jude and Aurelius were talking.

"How many other people in town were attacked by those demons?" Jude asked.

"We checked, and it appears no one. Everyone else seemed fine," Aurelius explained to him and anyone else who was listening. "We did a sweep. Those demons came straight to the inn. Whoever sent them knows we're staying here. It definitely wasn't a coincidence."

"Well, that's reassuring," Jude responded sarcastically. He then turned his attention to us and smiled. Maeve and I were both surprised by his reaction. She was telling me last night how he's warmed up to her now that he's seen her use her Veil Ki.

"Hey, Maeve," he said, holding out his hand and doing a handshake with her like they were old friends. She followed his lead on that and was equally as friendly.

"Jude. Everyone." She greeted.

"You nervous about today?" Jude asked her, still being nice, standing with his hands on his hips in his usual confident stance. "Because I sure as hell am."

You wouldn't even be able to tell. He seemed hyped and ready for whatever there was to expect.

Maeve nodded.

"Well, now that everyone is here," Aurelius said, pulling out the tablet with the map loaded on it, "let's start dividing into pairs of two."

Pairs of two? I thought, *how on earth was that supposed to be safe?*

"After the storm, our radar updated. Gwen and Caelum discovered that there could potentially be another hotspot. They are going to go check that one out. Jude, you and Soren will go here," Aurelius pointed at the map, "up the shore a ways but a little bit south, toward the outskirts of the woods and town. Maeve, you're with Ryu. You'll be going here, to the cliffside."

Ryu stood back like he already knew and had been

briefed prior to this meeting. It made me even more suspicious.

"Marina and I will stay here. We'll be on standby if any of you need medical attention or healing. Do not hesitate to call on us. Alright?" He looked around at everyone, making sure they were clear on his instructions.

Soren's mouth hit the floor. He didn't look too happy —in fact, a wave of disappointment washed all over him. It made me wonder if he was just as worried about Jude as I was about Maeve.

This plan that separated me from Maeve seemed deliberate. And to have a Veilkeeper at each hotspot where the portal could possibly be? Were they taking their chances—hoping to get either Jude or Maeve? Whichever one happened to be at the portal... is that the one that would have to die? Was Aurelius going to just let chance decide?

Were we really already there? Was he running out of options? And was there really a third hotspot that popped up, or were Caelum and Gwen ordered to stand by just in case something needed to be done and hard decisions were to be made?

I had so many questions that I wouldn't dare ask out loud. It felt as though my hands were tied. How was I supposed to help Maeve?

I looked over to see the expression on her face. She looked just as suspicious and uneasy about this arrangement and plan as I was. I could see it written all over her face. Neither of us trusted Aurelius in that moment.

I then turned my gaze to my brother, Ryu, who was partnered up with Maeve—thinking maybe I could read him and see if there was a sign or a clue of what to expect today.

Was he even given specific orders? What did Aurelius say to him, Gwen, and Caelum in the meeting last night? I should have been adamant about them letting me attend it as well, but the fact that Aurelius didn't seem to want me there only made me more suspicious that he was hiding something.

Ryu's expression: blank. He was my twin, so I should be able to read him, right?

Wrong.

He just stood. Hands in his pockets as usual, listening but staring off like he was bored.

"I don't like this plan," Soren spoke up. "I think I should stay here. Be the one to look after you and Marina. And I—"

"Come on, doofus," Jude said, pulling him by his ear and starting to walk away.

"Call us right away!" Aurelius called out after them as they were the first to head off in the direction of their assigned hotspot. "Maeve, you ready?"

She nodded. Ryu started to walk like he knew exactly where he was going.

I grabbed Maeve before she could follow him and pulled her into a tight hug. "Please call. Please. And be careful," I said, squeezing her tightly.

She hugged me back. I saw Ryu stop to wait—he turned slightly to glance over at us and then turned around, waiting for her.

"Ryu," I yelled out to him, "you better keep her safe."

He didn't respond.

Maeve kissed my cheek and then jogged up to him. They started walking, Maeve turning around to look at me one final time before they were making their way out of sight.

"We'll be going now too," Caelum said, he and Gwen walking off in a separate direction.

I waved at them and then stood there for a moment, processing what had just happened.

Aurelius walked up beside me—I could see him in the corner of my eye.

"Don't worry," he said. "She'll be fine with Ryu. I have my reasons for sending them together."

"I should have gone with her," I said weakly.

I felt Aurelius's eyes burning down onto me. "No, you shouldn't," he said coldly. His tone was flat.

"Will I ever see her again?" I asked in a defiant voice, obviously mad about his decision.

"I know what you're thinking," he replied. "You think I don't know you?"

I was shocked and taken aback. My breath hitched as I looked up at him and met his eyes. A serious expression on his face.

"I know you would kill Jude if it meant saving Maeve's life," he accused. "And I can't let you. My only plan today that you might not agree with is that you're staying here—with me—where I can see you."

I looked down. Guilty.

My eyes started to water. Not because of what he was saying—but because I was worried about Maeve.

I wiped my eyes and went back inside the inn to sit in the lobby. Aurelius wasn't going to let me go after her.

All I could do now was wait.

Chapter Thirty
Maeve

We hiked through the woods, but near the cliffside with an ocean view that was breathtaking—or maybe it was all the walking combined with the humidity that made it impossible to breathe. If it wasn't for the fact that I might be walking to my impending doom, I wouldn't have minded the hike so much. It was better than being deep in the woods, surrounded by tall, towering trees with who knows what hiding behind them.

I followed Ryu, as it seemed like he knew where he was going. I stayed alert, just waiting for those demons to come from out of nowhere. But this walk was peaceful.

Which freaked me out even more.

It was one of those *it's quiet... too quiet* kind of deals.

Ryu being on mute didn't help matters.

I've now only heard him talk just the one time—which caught me off guard. Nobody else responded the way I did, since they've heard his voice before.

I guess I'd already imagined how I thought he would sound, and it wasn't like that. His voice was sharp but smooth, controlled, raspy—with this icy bite to it. I don't even know if I'm explaining it right. I guess I could just go with the words *kind of sexy*. I kept these thoughts locked away. I didn't dare tell Marina, *wow, your twin's voice was replaying in my mind.*

I wanted to hear it again.

He stopped walking, and I got nervous. Worried that he was one of those demons that could hear what I was thinking. We were standing on top of a giant rock that had the woods behind us and the ocean in front. I looked back and saw the town—it looked so far away.

Ryu randomly sat down a few feet away from the ledge of the rock cliff. I looked down to see the waves crashing against the large rock formations and sharp pointed edges at the bottom. I would definitely be a goner if I slipped.

Since he sat down, I did the same. I gave him some space and sat a few feet away, on his right side.

He sat cross-legged. He crossed his arms and closed his eyes. I didn't know if he was stopping to meditate or taking a quick nap. So, I decided to ask.

"Uh," I started, "Are you meditating?"

Not a sound came from him. And he didn't look up.

I wasn't used to this cold shoulder, being-ignored treatment I was getting. Especially in my line of work. Normally, everywhere I go, people would stare, approach me, take photos of me—even if I was just trying to walk somewhere. Here, I was just a regular person. But to Ryu, I felt like I was nobody. I don't know why, but something about that drew me to him. It made me want to try harder to crack his shell.

Then it dawned on me.

We had been walking for a while now. Ryu wasn't using a map or calling anyone to ask for a reference on where to go. It was all so odd and peculiar. It made me wonder if Ryu was taking me out here for other reasons. Almost like we weren't even looking for a portal. Like there was an ulterior motive.

I started to wonder if that's why Aurelius separated me from the others and sent me with Ryu. Was it because he was the least likely to give a shit about sacrificing me if he had to? What if Aurelius had a choice to make, and this was it? Was this what their meeting was about last night?

I am the most useless Veilkeeper.

Auri sure as hell wasn't really going to leave which one of us dies up to chance.

He would choose to spare Jude. Jude deserved to be here and keep living more than me. He's saved the Earth way more times.

Maybe Auri had made his choice, and his intention today was to send Ryu out here to get rid of me. Dispose of me. Create the seal so they could all go home.

The thoughts rushing through my head started to affect me physically. And soon that thick air I'd been having trouble breathing in became damn near impossible. I jumped a little and swallowed hard, trying to catch my breath. I looked up—and had tunnel vision. My heart was racing. I knew what this was.

This was something I somehow managed to avoid feeling since I got here. But it was back now.

I was about to go into a full-blown panic attack.

I felt light—like any second now I was going to die. My hands and legs were shaking. I couldn't grasp anything. The ocean ahead—I tried to focus on it, but it felt like it, and the clouds, were moving slower than usual.

I was seeing them that way. I started to have a fear that I would suddenly lose consciousness.

The sky started to feel like it was falling. Falling right on top of my head. I tried to catch my breath and swallowed hard again as I jumped a little, still sitting, and ran my fingers through my hair, pulling it. I was moving like I was tweaking.

I quickly stood up—legs wobbly, shaking in fear. Gravity felt weird.

"I, uh—" I said, "I need to go. I need to head back now. I think."

My body's adrenaline was rushing. In this moment, I was in full flight mode. Like if I didn't get out of there soon, I was going to die.

Ryu opened his eyes, still sitting calm like always. Arms still crossed. He looked over and up at me.

"What's wrong?" he asked.

Too panicked to even care about him speaking again —I answered by saying, "Nothing. It's nothing. I just..."

And then it hit me.

My breathing was getting harder. My heart felt like it was beating so hard that it was just going to stop. I dropped to one knee, placing both my hands on the ground and hyperventilating. I felt like I only had seconds to live. Nothing felt real. My body felt light, floating. I couldn't feel my hands touching the ground even though they were. My vision— blurry.

"I'm dying," I cried. "It's happening right now!"

Something felt definite in my mind—that this was it. My brain couldn't simply be told otherwise.

I was in such a panic that I didn't even notice that Ryu had approached me. I felt him standing over me and saw his shadow under my hands. I looked up as he knelt down. He placed his hand on the back of my neck, under my long golden hair. His hand remained firm and in place—and then I started to feel something.

It was warm. Anchoring.

Like that feeling when you're sitting on a heated seat in a car. But it was on my neck. It felt like when you take that first sip of warm coffee. That cozy feeling—like you're being hugged.

It was his hand sending this feeling through me. It was distracting. My breathing started to settle. My heart rate leveled.

We stayed like that. I looked up as he stared towards the sea with those maroon eyes— they were just like Marina's.

I tried not to look at him and kept mine out on the water as well.

I started to relax.

He must've picked up on my energy calming down because he pulled his hand away and sat back, into a cross-legged position.

I sat on my bottom, knees drawn up to my chest,

hands together under them.

He turned to look at me, and we awkwardly made eye contact. I was embarrassed and looked away quickly.

He took his time before turning back to look off into the horizon. The ocean stretched endlessly.

I just sat and listened to the waves. The wind finally producing a slight breeze.

"Ryu…" I said softly.

I didn't expect him to respond. He was back facing the water completely, eyes closed, arms crossed. Meditating again, I guess?

"Ryu, I know you don't like to talk, but can you answer something for me?"

He opened one eye.

I know I had fear in my voice as I struggled to get the words out.

"Are you supposed to kill me?"

He turned to look at me completely—his eyes were now intense, penetrating. Felt like they were burning a hole through me. An unreadable expression on his face.

"I just mean—did Aurelius tell you to kill me if we found the portal? Am I going to die today?"

It looked like he rolled his eyes right before closing them again.

"No," he answered.

Short. Simple. Direct.

Just no.

I don't know why, but I believed him. Something about how he answered—even though it was one word—it was vague, but it was the truth. He wasn't lying.

What puzzled me was that Ryu always seemed like

he didn't care much about anything. It made me wonder why he was even here. Every time I saw him, he looked like he'd rather be somewhere else. So, I didn't understand why he was here saving the human world.

I sighed and wiped my eye from the tear forming.

"I'm not ready to die," I said out loud, without thinking. Not expecting him to respond.

"So don't die."

I looked at him—my face showing obvious shock. I think I looked that way every time he said anything.

He stood up again. "Ready?"

I nodded my head and kindly smiled. "Sure."

I helped myself up, not wanting to look any more needy.

He was an odd fellow, but deep down I think there was a lot more to him. I wanted to try to get to know him and see if he was anything like my Marina under his hard exterior.

I couldn't wait to head back to her once we were done exploring. I wanted to tell her what happened. How I had a panic attack on the edge of a cliff. How her brother got me through it.

But mostly—how he said, like a record of, seven words to me.

But honestly...

Who's counting?

Chapter Thirty-One
Jude

Soren complained the whole time we were walking. He was still mad that Aurelius paired me with him instead of Marina. No matter how many times I said, "Dude, just get over it," he still sulked.

"You know it's sad when you have to use a life-or-death mission as an excuse just to spend time with someone. You guys aren't even dating," I finally said to him.

He didn't even tell me to shut the hell up—just dragged his feet through the sand behind me like it was the end of the world. His anger was now turning into depression.

I exhaled and rolled my eyes. *Whatever.* His girl problems were the least of my worries. I was possibly about to be face to face with this portal thing—or more demons. And I only had Soren as backup.

Not to say Soren couldn't hold his own. My boy could always fight—especially thanks to Kosei's martial arts training. He'd been practicing with him for the past decade, and it's been helpful too. But Soren didn't possess

Veil Ki, and he wasn't a demon. He was unusually aware of the supernatural and could sometimes sense when spirits were around him. He was like a brother to me—my best friend—and honestly, it was nice having him around, at least when he wasn't being a pain in my ass.

We kept walking up the shore. We had to be close to this "hotspot," but since we'd been out here, there hadn't been a demon in sight.

"This is strange," I said and stopped walking.

Soren shook himself out of whatever thought he was having and stopped abruptly behind me.

"What is?" he asked.

"We've been out here for hours. And haven't been attacked by anything once."

"And that's a bad thing?"

"Where are all the big ugly monsters?" I looked around, the ocean water covering our feet and retreating back and forth as we stood and surveyed the area.

A few moments passed.

"Oh well. Portal must be closed. Time to go home," Soren joked.

"Ha ha," I commented dryly. He's so damn lame.

Then I noticed something up ahead.

"Wait—is that...?" I said, taking off in a brisk jog through the ocean-soaked sand. My feet pushed into the mush, trying to stay balanced as I ran toward what I saw.

What the hell is that?

"Jude! Wait for me!" Soren shouted after me as his big ass stumbled in the sand trying to keep up.

What I saw at first looked like a lump of seaweed

tangled in a mass of dark clothing. But when I got closer, I could see it for exactly what it was.

The body of a man.

Soren caught up and stood still next to me. His brain, like mine, actively processing what we were seeing right in front of us.

"Who is that?" he thought out loud.

I slowly approached, looking around to see if any of our favorite demon freaks were nearby. When I got closer to the body, I saw the man was face-down in the sand. His hair was matted with brine and grit.

"Ugh," I said, pulling my shirt over my face as a whiff of his faint, sickly odor mingled in the salt air. A rotten, decaying smell carried by the breeze straight to the back of my throat. I wanted to vomit.

Soren walked away coughing and gagging.

After the shock of the discovery started to wear off and I slowly returned back to reality, I noticed the sound of the restless pull of the waves and the gulls circling above us, screeching.

I could tell this dead guy had been here a while, and this kill didn't just happen. I didn't want to touch or turn him over to see how he died because I didn't want to alter any evidence for whatever investigation they'll do. But I assumed he fell victim to the demons we've been facing.

His clothes were soaked through. They clung to his lifeless frame like a second skin. His arms were awkward and sprawled—one twisted behind him while the other reached toward the dunes, like he was trying to grab something before he was killed.

"What the f— What kind of monster did this?" Soren muttered.

"I think we already know," I said, knowing he was just trying to make sense of what he was seeing.

I pulled out my phone and called Auri.

"Jude?" he answered on the first ring.

"Hey, uh... we found something."

"Is it the portal?" he asked, his voice tight with urgency.

"No," I said, turning to look at the dead, decomposing body behind me.

"Not exactly."

Chapter Thirty-Two
Maeve

It was starting to get dark. We had been searching all day in our assigned areas and found nothing. We thought there was a demon lurking at one point, but it appeared to be some kind of bear. Thankfully, it ran away—because if it had approached, I'm sure Ryu would've sliced it to shreds. Oddly, it seemed more afraid of him. Almost like it knew he was dangerous...and wasn't human.

"I don't sense anything. There's nothing. We searched the area high and low. There's no portal. Just woods now," I said, exhausted.

"They were here," Ryu suggested. "Perhaps the ones we have already slain."

"Oh," I said.

He turned to look at me with those eyes again.

I just looked down the moonlit shore off into the far distance.

And that's when I saw it—red flashing lights. Something was going on over there.

"What's that?" I wondered aloud, stepping closer in that direction, still unable to see clearly.

"Come on," he urged, starting to walk that way.

I didn't hesitate.

We broke into a run—down the hill and back toward the beach.

My heart was pounding again, my chest tightening as I worried it was someone from our team.

Chapter Thirty-Three
Soren

The local detectives arrived on the scene. Police blocked off the part of the beach where the body was discovered with caution tape. I overheard the detectives talking and saying it's strange how the body ended up way down here. It doesn't look like this is where he was killed, and if it weren't for the dead guy getting caught up in the rocks and the lower part of the dune where we found him, it's no small thing that he didn't get carried out to sea—and that his body would've never been recovered.

They were identifying him as the missing guy from town—Travis. But they'd still have to contact the next of kin and confirm, though it looked just like the guy who had gone missing a few nights back.

I saw Maeve and Ryu off to the side of the scene, standing behind the tape. Maeve waved us over. The detective was done taking our statements and said he'd contact us if there were any more questions.

Jude and I ran over to join Maeve and Ryu.

"We found Travis. The missing guy. He's dead," Jude informed.

Maeve's eyes grew large. "Travis?"

She looked toward the crime scene, where they were still huddled around his body and taking pictures.

"That's insane. Demons, right?" she asked.

"Hard to tell, but it has to be," Jude said.

"The only thing is they said it looked like Travis died from strangulation at first glance. He had marks on his neck. They weren't big or anything—just odd," I informed.

This made Ryu look up, his eyes stretching a bit, but then he returned to his normal composure like he didn't care. It was a sudden, short-lived, unexpected reaction from him—but I decided to just ignore it.

"Strangled?" Maeve asked, confused.

"Yeah," Jude confirmed. "Which Soren and I don't get, because the demons we've been fighting here are the tear-you-to-shreds-with-their-claws-and-teeth kind of monster."

"And then eat you for dinner," I added.

Jude nodded.

"Well, that doesn't fit," Maeve said, crossing her arms and then putting her index finger and thumb to her chin, visibly thinking this peculiar occurrence through.

"Travis didn't look like he'd been eaten. Except maybe from birds or smaller animals. Nothing like the shreds of remains we've found before," Jude said.

"This is just awful," Maeve said, holding her arms crossed, tightly against herself as the winds started to pick up.

"Well, I guess we should head back and inform the others," Jude said as we all started walking in the direction of the inn.

"Hey, stop!"

I heard a voice from behind. We all turned around to see one police officer wobbling toward us. It caught us off guard. I figured he just had more questions he wanted to ask.

"Hey—you're Daisy Maeve!" he said, pointing at Maeve.

Her face dropped, and she looked like a deer in headlights.

Busted.

"No," she managed to say. "I'm not."

"Yeah. Yeah, you are!" he said, pulling out his phone and showing us a picture of Maeve from a quick search on the internet. "I know what I see. This is you. My daughter listens to your music all the time. Plus, she's got a poster of you in her room."

We all looked at Maeve. She looked nervous. Like, *oh shit. We're done for*. The last thing this mission needed was a bunch of people flocking here once they heard there was a celebrity—someone as famous as her—nearby. This cop just blew our cover.

"I can see why you'd think that." Maeve spoke in a line that sounded like she's rehearsed it before. "But I'm not this Daisy person? My name is, uh—Jude Dee. It's Judy," she said.

I pressed my lips together, trying not to smirk and holding in a laugh at that. That's really all she could think of? The first name she pulled from the air.

"Come on," the cop said. "You think I'm dumb? You look identical to Daisy. You're her. Woah, this is crazy. And what are you doing out here at a crime scene? Man, I am going to be rich." He pulled out his phone and aimed the camera lens right at Maeve.

Jude was quick— stepping right in front of her as Maeve tried to cover her face.

"Don't you have anything better to do? Like, I don't know—your actual fucking job?" Jude snapped. "There's a dead guy literally laying ten feet from us and you're harassing my underage kid sister and asking her for pictures. Do I need to report you?"

"Yeah, what's your badge number?" I added, trying to sound noble. *Maybe Marina will hear about this.* Jude turned around and cut his eyes at me with a *Really?* look on his face. He knew my angle.

The chubby cop placed his phone back in his pocket and started stepping back. "I'm, uh... sorry to bother you kids." He wobbled back to the crime scene.

"Damn man, we showed no mercy on that cop! High five!" I put my hand up.

Jude just looked at me like I was the lamest person on the planet and walked away, sighing and shaking his head.

"Come on, guys," he said.

The four of us were heading back to the inn. I struggled to walk in the sand that wasn't as wet from the waves.

"So, you guys find anything today?" Jude asked Ryu and Maeve.

Maeve shook her head. "No. Nothing. Not even a demon."

"Yeah, besides Travis, I'm afraid we didn't have any luck either," Jude explained. "I wonder if Caelum and Gwen ran into any trouble."

I completely forgot those two were heading toward a third hotspot—one that was relatively newer than the ones we searched today. It made my stomach feel uneasy.

Mainly because of the dead guy's corpse that made me want to vomit again... but also because, if Jude and I didn't see any demons, and neither did Ryu and Maeve...

Then where were all the demons hiding?

What if Caelum and Gwen were ambushed?

I sensed now that something was wrong.

"Let's pick up the pace. We need to get back," I said.

"What?" Jude asked, confused. "What's your deal?"

Knot in my stomach, and my anxiety climbing, I told him ahead of time—half-truth to prevent him from thinking the worst.

"Nothing," I lied, but then admitted, "I just have a bad feeling."

Chapter Thirty-Four
Jude

We got back only to find Marina and Auri at the inn. They were sitting outside at one of those rusty metal tables and chairs you'd usually find in a garden. Marina was rocking anxiously, but her eyes shot toward us the second we approached. She jumped up and ran straight into Maeve, hugging her and holding her for a long time.

"Oh, my goodness, you're back!" she said, still tightly locked in an embrace—so tight that Maeve even struggled to hug her back because she couldn't move.

Maeve giggled. "It's okay, I'm alright, Marina."

Marina pulled away, wiping a tear from her eye. "I was so worried."

I looked to Auri. "Are Caelum and Gwen back yet?" I asked.

Auri stood and shook his head. "No. You all are the first ones here," he said as he walked toward us, a look of deep concern covering his face.

It hit me.

I don't know how I could be so stupid.

If the demons weren't at the two hotspots we checked, then it's possible Gwen and Caelum had a whole party of them waiting for them. They could be getting ambushed right now.

"We have to go find them!" I said urgently. "They might need our help!"

"Agreed," said Soren.

"Ryu?" I asked.

He nodded.

Just as we were about to take off—

"Hey, look over there!" said Maeve, pointing in the direction behind us.

I turned to see Caelum limping, Gwen holding him up as they walked toward us.

"Oh shit!" I exclaimed, and we all ran to them.

"What happened?" I ignorantly asked, already knowing damn well what probably went down.

"Demons," Caelum said weakly. Soren and Ryu grabbed him on each side to hold him up, Ryu taking over for Gwen.

Gwen stepped aside. "And not just one or two demons."

"Try thirty," Caelum muttered, about to pass out. Blood was trailing down the side of his head.

"We need to get him inside!" Marina shouted in a panic. "I can heal him!"

"Right," Soren agreed as they moved quickly but carefully.

Thirty demons. That's insane. That pretty much answered it—they were all partying at the newer hotspot. I had so many questions, but first thing was making sure Caelum was okay.

"Did you see the portal? Could you tell where they were coming from?" Auri asked.

"No, but it was definitely around there," Gwen answered.

Auri nodded. "I see. Let's get him upstairs."

"Damn, you're one tough bastard," I said once we got him to Auri's room. We laid him on one of the couches. He relaxed into it on his back, his deep red hair undone and messy from the fight, clothes torn. He placed one arm down and the other across his abdomen.

"Yeah, thirty demons is crazy. And all by yourself," Soren said in shock.

"It wasn't easy," Gwen said. "I wish I could have been more help, but I'm afraid I more so got in the way. Caelum was amazing, though. I didn't think we were going to make it out of there. You've become so powerful, Caelum."

"Well, thanks," he struggled to speak. "But not powerful enough... or I wouldn't be laying here like I got hit by a bus."

"Here," Marina said, putting her hands to his chest and closing her eyes. "This might hurt at first."

"Arghhh," Caelum grunted as her light-blue aura lit up his entire body.

I forgot about her healing powers. I'd seen them before when I was just a kid. The way it works is: first, you feel excruciating pain where you're injured—then she can manipulate the natural healing process to make it go a thousand times faster. It has to hurt before it gets better. At first, it's brutal, then the body eases, and you actually start to feel okay.

"Caelum?" Maeve spoke.

I turned to look at her. She looked horrified and was visibly shaking. I got up and walked toward her, pulling her arm gently and turning her away.

"Come on," I said, taking her out of the room.

The healing process wasn't like in the movies where the injured person lights up and *abracadabra* they're healed. It was brutal to watch if you weren't used to it.

Maeve and I walked into the hall. She put her hand up to her eyebrows, shielding her eyes.

"I'm sorry," she said. "I didn't mean to be weak in there. It's just—it's been a really long day."

"Yeah, no, I get it," I said.

Soren came out.

"He's going to be fine—it's just hard to watch," he said. "Also, I told Aurelius what the police said about Travis. He didn't seem all that surprised."

Yeah. I don't know. It was unfortunate, but I couldn't think any more about that dead guy. I needed a break from thinking about that dark shit.

Just then I had an idea. "Hey Soren, today's been nuts. Why don't we go grab a drink?"

"Nah, man," he replied. "No offense, but we spent the whole day together. I'm gonna go take a long shower and head to bed."

"Yeah, whatever. Go whack off in the shower, then." I rolled my eyes.

He was about to respond but looked too exhausted to

even argue. He just rolled his eyes and shook his head, heading off down the hall.

I turned to see Maeve's big eyes looking up at me.

She actually looked kind of... well, cute.

"What?" I asked, curious about that look she was giving me.

"I can go," she responded.

"Go where?"

"To drink with you."

"Uh," I said, rubbing the back of my head. Not sure if that was a good idea. I didn't really want to be seen with her, and the less she was out, the less likely we'd have a repeat of what happened today on the beach with that cop.

"Oh," she said softly, looking down. "I see. It's alright. I get it. I already know you don't like me."

HUH?

"Wow—wait a minute! Hold on!" I was caught off guard by how blunt she was being.

She balled her fist, something I notice she does a lot when she's upset and about to let out what she wanted to say.

"It's true. I know I'm a burden to you, Jude. I'll never, ever quite be as strong as you. And I know you don't want to be here working with me. So, I guess... why the hell would you ever want to hang out with me?"

She trailed off. I just looked at her—at a complete loss for words.

"Maeve—"

"I'll see you tomorrow," she said and started to turn down the hall.

"Hold on," I said, grabbing her wrist—surprising both of us.

She turned around. "Jude?"

I swallowed hard and looked into her eyes. "Do you want to—"

She stared at me, waiting for me to finish. She tilted her head.

"Let's go to the pub. Now. Together," I finished.

She smiled, but it quickly faded. "You don't have to."

"I want to," I said, cutting her off. "Come on."

We reached the pub. Maeve and I sat at the corner of the bar. The bartender, Jerry, didn't ID us. Maeve said it's probably because she'd been here before. This was the same place she met Travis—the guy we found on the beach. She also showed me the creepy portrait of Gladys hanging on the wall. I see now why she brought it up at one of the meetings. There was definitely something sinister about that whole story. Just the picture alone gave me chills.

"Aren't you a lovely couple," a woman at the bar leaned in and said. A man sat next to her. Neither of them were drinking—they looked early to mid-sixties.

"Oh, we're not—" I started, but the man cut me off.

"I met my wife right here, thirty-five years ago. Right down there on that beach. We've been together ever since. Makes me happy to see young folks here just as in love as we are."

Maeve was trying so hard not to laugh. She struggled to swallow her beer and set the glass cup down.

"You two are also a lovely couple," Maeve told the woman.

"Well, thank you," the woman said. "Now hold on—you look familiar."

Oh no. Here we go again.

The woman stared at Maeve and then hit her husband's arm. They both studied her.

Maeve tensed up next to me.

"Ah! I know," the husband said. "You were in here a few nights ago."

Maeve couldn't believe they remembered her just from that. But I could.

"It's not every day someone young like you comes in and just sits alone. The same tired people rotate through this bar every night," he explained. "I can tell you who's coming in and what time they'll be here. It's like clockwork."

"That's right, honey," the lady said. "When we saw you, we were surprised. We said, what a shiny new face."

"Did you two just move here?" the man asked.

"Oh no," Maeve replied. "Just visiting from out of town."

"I see," the man said. "Wanted some alone time? Somewhere it'd be just the two of you." He wiggled his eyebrows.

We just sat there. Neither of us could even conjure up a fake laugh.

I wanted to talk to Maeve without these bored people sitting here smiling and making small talk. I knew they were just being nice, but I wasn't in the mood.

Jerry walked over with a limp. He refilled the older

man's glass. It looked like the husband and wife were just drinking water.

"Carl, you hear about the man they found over on the beach?" Jerry asked. "Down at the very end?"

Carl shook his head. "Damn shame. Not surprised though. We try to warn these kids not to go out there at night. Here, keep the change."

The man pulled out a five-dollar bill that was torn at the top and threw it on the wet bar counter.

"I told you, water's free," Jerry laughed, but pocketed the money like there was no use arguing and he's told carl this countless times before. "Have a good night now," he said, waving at both of them.

They smiled and nodded at Maeve and me before walking out of the restaurant.

I prayed no one else would sit beside me. I turned to Maeve, putting my feet on the bottom rail of her barstool, fully facing her and blocking the seat next to me.

I looked up—and saw the eyes of the woman in the portrait. Gladys. Staring at me.

Maeve turned around to look at the picture, then back to me—clearly seeing it was bothering me.

I wasn't scared, but it was like the girl on the wall was trying to tell me something.

"Do you think she's out there right now?" Maeve asked, finishing the last of her beer. Jerry came over and brought her another without her even asking. Same tall glass. She picked it up and took a big ole sip before I noticed it was already halfway gone.

"Who?" I asked.

"The woman in the picture. Gladys."

I shrugged. But I wouldn't be surprised if what Maeve told me was true. That she might've seen her walking around one night. Ghosts aren't as uncommon as normal people might think.

"Being a Veilkeeper," I started, "I've seen some shit. But I will admit—ghosts are hard to fight."

She nodded, a little energetic now from the temporary beer buzz. "One day we'll have to sit down and really compare stories."

I smiled. I liked that idea. I'd never spoken to another Veilkeeper before except Kosei. I wondered if Maeve had to go through the same process I did—and what growing up fighting evil really looked like for her. I've seen she's got moves. But I'd love to hear about her bad guys. Her favorite power moves. Just her outlook on life in general.

Kosei has accepted his life as a Veilkeeper. He never settled down romantically. Said our lives are too unpredictable. He's right. There's a good chance one or both of us might die—possibly tomorrow.

I chugged the remainder of my drink just thinking about it.

"They really thought we were dating. We must look like we get along well," Maeve said.

"Hey," I replied. "We get along just fine."

"So," she said, her eyes gleaming, "you don't hate me?"

Hate was a strong word. I'll admit—at first, I didn't care too much for Maeve. I still don't really know her. But I know that I don't dislike her, either.

"You're cool."

She smiled and finished her drink. "What time is it?"

I checked my pockets. "Drats—I must've left my phone in my other clothes."

Before we came here, I felt gross in the clothes I was wearing when we found dead Travis. Maeve and I went by my room first before coming out. I changed my pants and jacket, and my phone must've gotten left behind.

"Don't worry about it," she said. "Let's pay and head back."

We finished our beers and walked back to the inn together. I helped her step over the remaining glass shards at the front of the inn—which still hadn't been blocked off. We laughed about how that door's probably never getting fixed and how much of a safety hazard it is.

We rode the elevator up. She got off on floor two. She turned and waved with a huge grin as the doors closed. I returned the same expression.

She really was alright. I didn't mind her at all.

I got back to my room. I shut the door slowly because I could hear Soren snoring the second I walked in. I went straight over to my pants on the floor and pulled out my phone.

I clicked it on.

And my heart sank into my stomach.

It read that I had missed calls.

All seven of them.

From Kayo.

Chapter Thirty-Five
Maeve

I got off the elevator on the second floor but decided I wasn't ready to go sit in my room. Especially after feeling so buzzed from the alcohol Jude and I drank at the pub. I stumbled back down the stairs and out the back door to the lower deck of the inn, overlooking the beach on the bottom floor. I went over to the rail and looked down the beach toward the ocean.

No sign of Gladys...

I *swear* I saw her ghost that one night, but what if it was just a girl out for a stroll?

No way. Those old clothes, the glowing skin, the matted hair hanging in her face?

"It had to be a ghost," I whispered out loud to myself.

I sighed and turned to go back into the inn. But then I didn't feel so great. I went over to one of the chairs sitting by the covered pool and sat down, wrapping my arms around my stomach and staring at my feet. The deck appeared to be spinning.

Did I really drink that much?

I was nervous around Jude at the pub.

Suddenly, I looked up—and it wasn't just my feet I was seeing. Another pair of shoes appeared in front of me. I recognized the sleek, black, slender boots. They weren't the type normal human boys would wear.

It was Ryu.

I slowly looked up to see him standing over me, red eyes gleaming again—not the soft maroon from earlier today.

"Ryu," I greeted, then went back to rocking.

"You shouldn't be out here," he told me, like a warning.

"How did you know?" I asked.

He looked up, and my eyes followed his.

"I was sitting on my balcony. I saw you down here."

I giggled.

He didn't find it amusing. But all I could think about was how he must've jumped down. I didn't even notice. I hadn't been here long enough for someone—even with his speed—to get here that fast.

"Did you *jump*?" I asked flat-out.

He nodded, then uncrossed his arms. I noticed he didn't have the scary back-mounted fire daggers tonight. Still, he was intimidating.

"Ryu, I—" I started, but suddenly, the world tilted again. My stomach turned, and I knew nothing I did was going to stop it.

That alcohol was coming back up. Fast.

I darted to the railing and threw up over the side of the deck.

It was disgusting.

It just kept coming, like I was some kind of possessed creature losing all control.

"Gross..." I whimpered between vomiting.

Too ashamed to look back and see Ryu's reaction, I stayed facing forward.

Then, a towel appeared beside me.

One of those old, dirty pool towels. God knows how long they'd been sitting there. Folded on one of the tables, rained on, full of sand and who knows what else. The pool was covered, so no idea what the towels were even still doing out here.

I took it anyway. It was better than having vomit dripping from my mouth and chin.

This was *so* embarrassing.

First, the panic attack in front of Ryu. Now I was out here barfing everywhere like a little kid. He had to think I was the worst. He probably hated me more than he disliked Soren.

"Thank you," I mumbled without making eye contact. I wiped my face and tossed the towel aside, going back over to the chair and putting my head in my hands. All I could hear was the ocean.

I wasn't even sure if he was still standing there.

"You should go upstairs," he suggested.

"I can't," I told him. "Marina's going to smell how bad I reek of alcohol."

"So," he said.

I looked up and saw him shrug. I laughed.

He was so cute.

And then, I don't know how I managed to conjure the courage, but I asked him:

"Can I shower in your room?"

It *had* to be the alcohol, but even as innocent as I meant it, I knew it wasn't something I'd normally ask. Still, I was surprised by his reaction.

He didn't flinch.

He shrugged again. "If you want."

I smiled—probably bigger than I planned to.

He turned and started walking toward the stairwell. I got up, still dizzy, but nowhere near as bad, and followed him. Once inside, I clutched the stair rail for dear life as I started to feel nauseous again, but I powered through.

He turned to look at me—so casual, so cool.

I gave him a bright, toothy smile. "I'm okay. Nothing to see here."

He just shook his head.

I was so surprised he was letting me go up to his room. Maybe he didn't hate me after all.

We passed Jude and Soren's room, then reached Room 309. I had a quick flashback of being here before, back when I got the room numbers mixed up.

He swiped his key card and let us in.

The lights were still on. I followed him in and shut the door behind me.

I looked down to check if I had vomit in my hair or clothes—thankfully, no. But I realized I had nothing to change into.

"Can I borrow a shirt? Maybe some pants for after? I know they'll be big on me, but I promise I'll give them back."

He closed his eyes and nodded.

"Thanks," I said, and disappeared into the bathroom, closing the door behind me.

I started the shower to let it heat up. When I looked in the mirror... I looked rough. Tired mostly, but the alcohol was amplifying my ratchetness.

Ugh. Why do I always look like hell in front of a cute guy?

I've been all dazzled up for award shows—and someone like *Ryu?* Nowhere to be found.

He was *so* rare.

And then it hit me, as I dropped my clothes and saw myself in the mirror.

I think I want Ryu to be my first.

I mean—think about it. He's basically the guy version of Marina, my best friend. He helped me through a panic attack. He's strong, handsome, cool. And he doesn't care how famous I am. He wouldn't use me.

Also—he knows I'm a Veilkeeper. That means something.

He was... perfect.

I got in the shower and rinsed off. I shampooed my hair, washed with soap—nothing fancy. Just the standard existential overthinking that happens in the shower.

Why would he want me?

He saw me vomit.

He saw me panic.

He probably thinks I'm pathetic.

Ryu probably has demon girls—way stronger than me—throwing themselves at him.

Why would he want weak, human *me?*

I got out of the shower and wrapped myself in a towel. I told myself:

I'm going to be brave.

Who cares if I embarrass myself? I already have, several times. And if I die tomorrow...

I walked to the sink. Unwrapped one of the backup toothbrushes and used the sample toothpaste. I brushed my teeth and freshened up.

Okay, you got this. Worst he can say is no.

I opened the bathroom door, took a deep breath. The minty scent still lingered as I stepped into the room with just my towel on.

There was a navy-blue shirt, and hunter-green sweatpants folded neatly at the edge of the bed. I was surprised he owned anything that wasn't black.

Ryu sat in the corner chair, diagonally near the balcony door, sharpening one of his daggers.

My heart sank.

Was he about to use that on me? The seal *does* require blood...we think.

But wait—why would he give me clothes if he was going to stab me?

He noticed the look on my face and gestured toward the clothes with the sharpening tool.

He's not going to hurt me.

"Ryu," I said, stepping closer. I stood by the bed, only the towel on.

I wanted to talk but couldn't find the words.

He looked at me—confused. Raised an eyebrow.

"What are you doing?" he finally asked.

"I... uh..." I stammered. My sober self was coming back, and this suddenly felt like a *very* bad idea.

"I put clothes over there," he said, nodding to the bed.

"I, well—Ryu..." I trailed off again.

He looked at my legs. Scanned up to my eyes.

His confusion turned to something else.

Indifference.

Like he genuinely couldn't care less.

So, I just... blurted it out.

"Ryu, I want to do it!"

I grabbed my face in embarrassment... and forgot I was holding the towel up.

It dropped.

Bare. Ass. Naked. In front of him.

Damn.

I kept my eyes covered.

He sighed. Then laughed.

It was the strangest laugh—cool, but with a little edge.

I peeked through my fingers. Cheeks burning. Eyes tearing up.

He got up, walked over, and handed me the shirt and pants.

"Here," he said.

That answered that.

He wasn't interested.

I wanted to sink into the floor and *die*.

I grabbed the clothes and put them on as quickly as possible, trying not to cry. He walked in front of me and gently placed both hands on my shoulders.

I wasn't expecting it.

He guided me to sit down on the bed near the balcony. Sat across from me. One leg on the bed, the other on the floor. Still facing me. Still calm.

"You need to get some sleep," he said.

"Yeah," I tried to play it off. "I'm just going a little crazy. Beer does that."

He pulled his hands away but stayed in front of me.

I looked down. "I'm not your type, huh?"

Silence.

Then he said, "Not this version of you, no."

"...What does that mean?" I asked.

"I don't want to do anything with you," he said, then added, "while you're drunk."

My face turned red again.

He said *while I'm drunk.*

Either he didn't want to hurt my feelings... or maybe... there was a chance?

"I'm not that drunk," I argued. "I threw up most of it."

Nice, Maeve. Real sexy. I thought in my head.

He walked over to his daggers again. I tensed up.

"I'm not going to use these on you."

"Oh, that's good news," I said awkwardly.

"Why do you do that?" he asked while re-strapping his weapons.

"Do what?"

"Act so nervous around me?"

Uh, because you don't talk, and you move different than anyone I've ever met. Also—you're a demon.

None of that came out. Instead, I just said, "Because I like you."

He paused. Then went to close the balcony doors. As if giving himself time to respond.

Then he said, "I know."

"What?" I thought.

Well, duh, Maeve—you did just throw yourself at him.

"I think you should sleep," he repeated.

Without even asking, I crawled into his bed.

He didn't stop me. So, I assumed that meant I could.

He turned off the lights, then sat down on the opposite side. He didn't lay down—just leaned back against the headboard, arms behind his head, relaxed. Eyes closed.

I got up and scooted closer to him, sitting in front of him. Close—but not in his lap.

"Ryu..." I whispered. "Do you like me too?"

It was dark, but I swear he smiled.

I laughed and covered my face. "Oh my gosh. I need to stop. You're just being nice."

He pulled his hands down and grabbed my wrists gently.

"Stop that," he said. "No more being nervous around me."

"Okay," I whispered.

He smiled. "Good girl."

OH HOLY COW! He *did not* just say that.

I was instantly turned on.

I leaned forward and kissed him. I didn't think he'd kiss back—

But he did.

His hand touched my leg. His other hand went up

behind my head, pulling me in more and delicately grabbing some of my hair. I melted into it.

"Ryu," I whispered. "I've never done it before. And I might die soon."

His grip tightened slightly.

"You're not going to die. I won't let that happen."

Was he being nice? Or did he actually care?

Regardless, I asked again, "Can we please?"

This time, without hesitation—he kissed me.

It was perfect. Slow. Aligned.

I climbed into his lap. His hands explored, but gently. Nothing rough. It wasn't aggressive—it was passionate.

He pulled away and looked me dead in the eyes.

"You're not going to die."

"I might."

"You won't," he said. "Now I want you to sleep."

He was bossy in a caring way—like Marina.

I pouted.

That made him smile.

"None of that. Another time. When you're sober. And certain."

"I *am* sure."

"And not haunted by your mortality."

"...Okay. You got me there."

I laid down and snuggled next to his lap. He remained sitting upright.

"Goodnight," I whispered.

I felt his hand rest gently on my back.

It was the safest I'd felt in days.

He stayed the perfect gentleman.

And all of this?

It just made me like him that much more.

Chapter Thirty-Six
Jude

Today felt like it was *it*. I woke up with a strange feeling in my gut.

Something was going to happen.

I was sure of it.

I tried calling Kayo back a hundred times. No answer.

I texted her: *I'm sorry. I didn't have my phone.*

I decided to call one last time—and to my surprise, she answered.

"What, Jude?"

"Kayo, listen—"

"Oh, *now* you have time for me."

"Dude, I always have time for you. I was busy. Yesterday a lot happened."

I was already getting tired of her jealous behavior while I was out here literally standing face to face with death.

"Where were you last night?" she snapped. "After everything you told me, I was worried sick!"

"I'm fine." I sighed. "Yesterday we found a dead body on the beach. Then Caelum was attacked. He got messed up pretty bad."

"Oh my god—Is he okay?" Her tone shifted to panic.

"He's gonna be fine. Marina used her healing powers, so it should speed up his recovery."

"Oh, Jude, I'm so sorry," she said, softening. "I shouldn't have been so mean about it."

I sighed again and rubbed my face with one hand while still holding the phone in the other. I had to tell her the rest.

"I was so stressed out about everything... I did go and have a few drinks," I admitted.

"Oh," she said. "I mean, I get it? I think. You saw a lot yesterday. Who did you go drink with? Was it Soren?"

I took a deeper breath.

Contemplated lying.

"No. Maeve."

"Oh, you went with Maeve. Oh, so you couldn't answer my calls while I was losing my mind because you were too busy out on a date! Just like I *said* you would be! *With her!*"

Kayo started yelling. I pulled the phone away from my ear.

"It wasn't a date!" I said.

It wasn't. I didn't even see Maeve like that. It wasn't a date.

"What else did you do?" she asked, accusing.

"What?"

"Well, you're scared you're going to die. You're alone

with a girl that understands you and is gorgeous. What else happened?" She wouldn't stop.

"Nothing! What the hell!" I yelled, turning around to see Soren sit up, groan, and then lay back down, pulling a pillow over his face. He must've still been wiped from all the walking we did yesterday. Honestly? Between that and the beers, I wasn't in the best shape this morning either. And now I had to deal with Kayo losing her shit over something that didn't happen.

"You two went to get drunk alone. You didn't call me back till this morning. I know what happened, Jude. You had sex with her."

"No, I didn't!" I shouted.

I didn't mean to yell, but it was frustrating. I could see what it looked like—but I didn't touch her.

"Jude, you know what? Don't call me anymore. Go have fun with her. You guys can go die together. It'll be so romantic, just like the cheesy storybooks we read when we were kids."

"Kayo, don't do this." I was begging now. The last thing I needed was her being mad at me.

"Goodbye, Jude. You made your choice."

"Kayo, stop!" I shouted louder.

"Jude, shut up," Soren groaned from under the pillow.

And then—

A knock.

A loud one.

"JUDE!"

The girl's voice came through the door.

Loud enough that somehow Kayo heard it too.

"Oh, your girlfriend's already up and ready for more. Guess you have to go," she spat.

"JUDE! SOREN! WAKE UP!"

The yelling and knocking continued.

I recognized the voice now—so did Soren.

It was Marina.

And she sounded scared.

I carried the phone with me, Kayo still yelling on the line, as I followed behind Soren who rushed to open the door.

Marina stood there, eyes wide, panicked.

"It's Maeve! She's gone! I can't find her anywhere!" she cried.

A knot twisted in my stomach.

I saw her get off the elevator on the second floor...

Did something happen in the time it took me to get back to my room?

I was so exhausted after the bar, I just crashed.

Figured she did the same.

This is all my fault.

I was the last one with her.

"Jude? JUDE!" Kayo's voice shrieked from the phone still in my hand.

I looked at Marina—her eyes filled with tears.

Soren stood frozen, watching her cry hysterically.

I felt anger boil over.

At myself.

At Kayo.

At everything.

Maeve might need me—and here I was caught up

in petty relationship drama with someone who clearly didn't understand me anymore.

Neither Maeve nor I chose this life.

But Kayo doesn't seem to get that. She used to.

Now? All she saw was betrayal. Jealousy. Bitterness.

Maybe she was right.

Maybe she didn't really understand what it meant to be a Veilkeeper.

But Maeve did.

"Kayo, believe whatever the hell you want," I snapped, and hung up.

I had to find Maeve.

She couldn't have been that drunk.

Maybe she just went for a walk.

Or maybe...

Worse.

Maybe she wandered near the portal.

Maybe the demons came back.

"We'll find her," Soren said, comforting Marina.

I threw on my jeans. "I'm going to wake Ryu up. He'll help."

"Right," Soren nodded. "Come on, Marina, let's go tell Aurelius and Gwen."

The two of them took off for the stairs.

I jogged down to Ryu's room and knocked like I was the police.

Not that he was a deep sleeper—I just couldn't stop panicking.

My mind was racing.

Was she taken? Attacked? Were more demons here?

I should've walked her to her room.

The door flung open—

But it wasn't Ryu.

It was Maeve.

Wearing Ryu's oversized clothes.

My eyes went wide.

Every ounce of panic left my body like air escaping a balloon.

Maeve looked like a deer in headlights—like she'd been caught sneaking cookies before dinner.

I tried to hold it in, I really did.

But I burst out laughing.

"Shut up! Stop—it's not funny!" she said, laughing too, but clearly flustered.

I snickered. "Oh my gosh, you are wild. Hey Ryu!"

"Shush!" Maeve pushed into me, stepping out into the hall and quickly closing his door behind her—accidentally locking herself out.

"Oops," I joked, laughing again.

"Jude! Quiet! Where's Marina?"

"Upstairs. Telling Auri you're missing."

"Crap!"

"Yeah, I'll say. Now everyone's going to know you were doing the dirty with her brother last night." I grinned. "Dang, Maeve. How did you pull that one off?"

She was scrambling, looking around in a panic. I didn't see why it was such a big deal.

I was just relieved that she was okay.

"Marina is going to see me dressed like this!" she whispered, tugging at her oversized shirt.

"Well, if you hurry, you can run back to your room and change before she comes back down."

She looked hopeful. But then—

"Your secret will be safe with me," I added with a wink.

"Jude, I can't! I don't have the room key! She's going to see me and—"

Before she could finish, the stairwell door swung open again.

Auri, Gwen, Soren, and Marina all stepped out.

Maeve froze.

Right in front of me.

In Ryu's clothes.

Everyone was staring.

Busted.

Chapter Thirty-Seven
Marina

"I was worried sick!" I yelled at Maeve once we were back in our room.

She walked from the bathroom and sat on the corner of the bed. She had changed out of my brother's clothes and back into hers. She wore tan shorts and a thin shirt with a cropped halter top underneath. I watched her as she bent over and started putting on her combat-style boots.

"I'm fine," she replied, but I could tell by her tone that I was getting on her nerves. She clearly didn't want to talk about what happened last night.

"How was I supposed to know that? With everything going on... you didn't think to at least send me a text letting me know you weren't lying out there somewhere *dead*?" My words came out sharp. "You saw what happened to Caelum!"

"I know, Marina. I'm sorry."

Unbelievable. I wasn't even sure what I wanted her

to say—there *wasn't* anything she could say that would undo how scared she made me feel.

"Whose clothes were those?" I pressed.

She threw her head back and let out an exaggerated pout.

"Ryu's."

"Ryu? *As in my twin brother, Ryu?* Why on earth were you wearing *his* clothes?"

I wasn't sure I even wanted to hear the answer.

She looked around the room suspiciously, like she had something to tell me but didn't know how to say it.

"He didn't... did he?"

"No," she answered quickly.

"Well, it's just that Jude said the two of you had been drinking—which, don't even get me started on that part—"

"No," she said again, running both hands through her hair. "It was fine."

"What was?" I asked. "Did he have sex with you?"

"No!" Her face turned as red as I'd ever seen it. "We didn't. We just kissed... and he held me. It was nice."

I was shocked.

First of all, forget the fact that she was *hooking up with my brother*—which, honestly, I didn't find too weird. If I had to pick a guy for her, Ryu wasn't a bad choice. He wasn't the nicest guy in the world, but it sounded like he didn't take advantage of her.

"He wouldn't go any further," she explained. "I mean, I tried—because I was intoxicated—but he was so respectful, Marina. I really think..." she trailed off, "...if it's okay—I think I like him. A lot."

I sighed and paused.

"Maeve, *of course* it's okay."

"Really?"

"Yes. And I'm glad you told me."

We both sat quietly, taking all this in. She then began to tell me the whole story. Some of it didn't even sound like my brother at all.

"Wow," I said with a small grin. "I can't say I saw this coming. I never knew he had it in him."

"What do you mean?"

"Well... I mean being so *open* with you."

"Me neither. I didn't even think he liked me."

"Of course he likes you," I said.

"Well... you know. He wouldn't talk to me. He was always so quiet."

"He's like that with *everybody*, Maeve. He isn't much of a talker. I *told* you that before."

She smiled like she was replaying everything from last night in her head, then bit her lip.

"Maeve..." I said cautiously.

She just kept smiling and sat there quietly.

I saw it written all over her face. This was a new feeling for her. She'd never had anything like this before —and right before my eyes, I was watching my best friend fall in love.

"All right," I finally said, "Aurelius wants us downstairs soon. Let's get through today and whatever this mission ends up being... and then we can start figuring out what to do about you and Ryu."

"Me and Ryu?" she asked.

"Of course! You're going to want to see him again after all this is said and done, aren't you?"

"Yeah... but Marina, you know how it is."

"No, I don't. Tell me."

"My parents. They would *never* allow it."

I gave her a tight smile as I watched her excitement dim, like she was falling back into that sad reality where her parents run and rule her entire life. Always holding everything over her head.

We'd already spent a lot of time in Starbrook. It was only a matter of time before they started calling again. Wondering where she was.

Maeve was just like the girls in the fairytales—the princess with royal duties and suffocating parents. But then she met a guy who acted like a real prince. Kind. Patient. Someone who didn't force her into anything and accepted her for who she was, even when she was a mess. He saw her anxiety. Saw her puke. And still? He was *kind*.

He gave her a small piece of himself—something I know my brother doesn't give away easily.

There was *something* about Maeve that intrigued him. Not just her beauty. Something else. Something about her light that pulled in the most closed-off guy I know.

Ryu didn't want to take from her.

He wanted to *protect* her.

That feeling?

I knew it too well.

"We'll figure it out," I said—the famous words I always say to her when she's filled with doubt.

"You always say that," she countered.

"Well, because it's true," I said, chuckling. "Doesn't it always work out?"

"Yeah... somehow."

"Well then listen to me—it *will* work out. We'll get through everything here. And we'll deal with your parents. Together."

She gave me a faint smile.

"Now come on, let's go. We're going to be late," I said, walking over to her and placing my hands on her shoulders.

She smiled. Her eyes widened like she just had a thought, then softened again—her expression changing into something steady and confident.

"Okay," she said. "I'm ready."

Chapter Thirty-Eight
Aurelius

The plan was to close the portal today.

Gwen had the medical supplies. She and Soren were sitting on the couch in the lobby, organizing everything into the giant satchels. We had Marina—her healing powers would come in handy. Though I still needed to keep my eye on her. Her loyalty lay solely with Maeve, and I knew that if it came down to it, she'd make the choice for us without hesitation.

I spoke to her brother, Ryu. He's watching her too.

This was what I wanted to discuss the night the demons attacked the inn. I didn't want Jude to hear that Marina might be plotting to kill him if it meant saving Maeve. So, I only asked to speak with Caelum and Ryu in private.

I know I'm losing trust among the Veilkeepers. The Spirit World has always harbored secrets behind their backs—but I owed it to those two to be honest.

I would talk to them both again once they came

downstairs. I wouldn't rush them—if I were in their place, I wouldn't be rushing either. But today *had* to happen, one way or another.

My goal is to walk away from this day with *both* of my Veilkeepers still breathing.

If I had to choose.

The truth is—I chose *both*.

Caelum was still upstairs resting. As much as we needed his help, I didn't want to risk him any further. He'd already done more than enough. Gwen said he took out the majority of the demons the night they attacked— and he did it almost singlehandedly. But we weren't quick to celebrate. The portal was still open. Whoever was behind all of this would just send more.

Eventually.

Jude and Ryu appeared downstairs.

"We checked on Caelum," Jude reported. "He's still pretty banged up but said if we really need him, he'll show up. I told him to just rest and try to regain whatever energy he's got left."

I nodded. "That's what I was thinking too. Thank you, Jude, for letting me know."

He nodded once, then sat on the couch across from Gwen and Soren, staying out of the way.

The elevator doors swung open—and out came Marina and Maeve. Neither of them made eye contact. Both of them looked lost in their heads, drowned in anxiety and quiet thought.

Soren lit up at the sight of Marina and jumped to his feet.

"Careful!" Gwen shouted, reaching for him, but it was too late.

Everyone watched in horror as Soren's foot got caught in the strap of one of the med satchels. He went flying forward, tried to catch himself, and instead—

smashed straight through the glass table.

Glass *exploded* everywhere. It happened so fast, none of us had time to stop it.

Marina's eyes went huge. She rushed over, trying to help but avoiding the scattered shards as best she could. Ryu moved quickly and helped her get Soren upright. Gwen checked the bag for broken supplies.

Jude slapped his hand over his face and sank into the couch.

"You see? *This* is why I didn't want to bring you," he groaned.

Referring to the mission.

Soren, now standing but clearly a mess, winced. "I'm okay," he said—but blood trickled from a cut on his forehead, and he was staggering.

"Let's go sit down," Marina said, guiding him over to the table and chairs by the window.

I scanned the lobby. The front door and windows were still broken from when the demons stormed in that night. Now glass littered the floor from the shattered table. We were destroying this place piece by piece.

Great. Now all I had was Jude, Ryu, and maybe Maeve as fighters. Soren needed medical attention—and fast.

Gwen unzipped a first aid kit and hurried over.

Marina joined, using her healing powers carefully—I could tell she was trying to conserve them.

"You're such an idiot," Jude called out from across the room.

"Hey!" Soren snapped. "You're not the one covered in fucking glass!"

"Hold still," Gwen muttered as she pulled a shard from his arm.

I shook my head.

Then I looked to Maeve.

She was off to the side. Distant. Still staring into nothing. She hadn't said a word.

I wasn't the only one who noticed. Ryu glanced at her, too.

But Maeve was lost in her own world.

I walked over to her. "Maeve, a word," I said. Then turned and signaled Jude to follow us. Everyone quieted as the two of them trailed behind me out onto the back deck.

The ocean was loud today. Louder than usual. Waves crashed against the shore like they were trying to warn us. The air was thick and salty. The wind strong.

I turned around. My Veilkeepers looked at me, waiting.

Maeve tried to keep her hair out of her face. Jude stood with arms crossed—classic.

Looking at them, I couldn't help but remember when they were just children. They hadn't changed much. Taller. Older. Somewhat more mature. But still the same kids who were called to be Veilkeepers all those years ago.

I sighed—and laughed a little.

They both looked confused.

"I don't see what's funny," Jude said.

"Is it my hair?" Maeve asked, still fighting the wind.

"No, it's not that," I said, wiping at my eyes. It was sand. Not tears I swear.

"It's just... you two have come so far. You've survived every challenge. You're still here. Still standing."

"We had help," Maeve mumbled, looking down. The self-doubt always waiting.

"You *have* help now," I replied. "You have each other."

They exchanged a glance.

"This whole time I thought splitting you up was safer. But I see now... I was wrong. I didn't split up the team. I delayed the team from forming. But now that you're together—we'll get through this."

"You're oddly positive," Jude said.

"Yeah, it's making me uncomfortable," Maeve added, grinning a little.

"No really," I said again, "It's all going to work out. But I want you two to stick together today. Please."

Another glance passed between them.

And then I realized: I'd waited almost a decade to bring them together. They should've met years ago. They'd be synced up by now. Familiar with each other's style—fighting, personality, even trust.

This was on me.

I never meant to keep them apart, but I did.

And it might cost us everything.

"Alright," I said, clearing my throat. "Today, we stick

together. We work as a team. No splitting up. After we clear the demons and perform the ritual, one of you might have to be cut—but don't worry. We have supplies and Marina's healing powers. You'll be fine."

"This is what you pulled us aside to tell us?" Jude asked, unimpressed. "I thought it was going to be some top-secret, confidential mission intel."

"What? I—"

I looked at Maeve. She had her arms crossed too now, equally disappointed.

"I just wanted to look at you both and say it's going to be okay. Plus, I—"

"Oh no," Jude cut in. "Is this the part where you say you love us and how proud you are?"

He looked at Maeve. She giggled.

I rolled my eyes. "Sure."

"Then say it," Maeve pushed.

My face turned red. "You know I'm proud of you both. Now come on, let's get going. The others are waiting."

"Yeah, yeah," they muttered, turning and walking back toward the building—*in sync.*

It was true. If you knew them before this chapter in their lives, you'd know how far they've come. How much they've survived.

Did I really believe everything would be okay?

No.

Not at all.

I didn't know if the plan would even work.

But I needed to see them one more time. The two I

had watched grow up. The two I was now expected to sacrifice.

I needed to look them in the eyes before all hell broke loose.

And I potentially lost one of them.

Or both.

Chapter Thirty-Nine
Jude

The forest was unnaturally still.

Closer to the inn, the wind had been whipping like crazy—Maeve kept getting smacked in the face with her own hair, and Auri was supposedly getting sand in his eyes.

I think he was crying, but I wasn't about to call him out for it. It was kinda nice to see someone from the Spirit World actually *gave a shit* that we might die today.

I held my breath—but not on purpose—as me, Soren, Auri, Gwen, Maeve, Marina, and Ryu walked along the trail toward the area where Gwen and Caelum had been attacked yesterday. There wasn't a shred of doubt in Gwen's mind that the portal was nearby. The way the demons rallied around it like a damn party. Yeah, I'd say she was right.

The trees turned stiff. Not even the leaves moved. No birds. No sounds.

Something was ahead. I could feel it.

I turned to look at Ryu to see if he was getting the same vibes.

He gave me a single nod.

Yeah. We were close.

Gwen, leading the way, started to slow down. Auri moved up beside her, walking in sync. She was still shaken from what she'd seen the day before.

Maeve walked behind Soren and Marina. Soren stayed really close to Marina—maybe he was sensing something too, or maybe he just wanted to look like a tough guy. I wasn't sure.

Gwen came to a full stop, scanning the area. Auri's eyes narrowed, then turned to her.

She nodded. "This is where Caelum and I were attacked."

We all froze.

Everyone stopped walking.

There was this eerie silence after our footsteps halted.

I looked up. The sun was peeking through the towering trees surrounding us, but I still felt like we were locked in. Trapped.

I felt surrounded.

"I don't like this," Soren said.

So he felt it too.

They were here.

The demons were watching us.

We instinctively formed a circle—backs to each other —eyes on the tree line.

Crack.

A sharp sound shattered the silence. A flash of silver shot from the trees like lightning.

"Maeve!" Gwen shouted.

The jagged, spear-like object flew toward Maeve's face, but Ryu was faster.

He tackled her just in time. The sharp object sailed past and slammed into a tree on the opposite side, embedding itself deep into the trunk.

"What the hell was that?" Soren yelled, shielding Marina with his arm.

Ryu hovered over Maeve, still on guard. His eyes never left the shadows.

"Ryu..." Maeve's voice trembled as she sat up a little, trying to see his injury. She pulled gently on his arm. His cloak had been grazed by the projectile, and he was bleeding.

He pushed her back down—not rough, just firm—his eyes scanning the trees.

"Stay down," he growled, tone even grumpier than usual.

Then something emerged from the trees.

It wasn't like the demons we'd been fighting.

This one was taller, *beige* instead of white. Like an apex version. An orca compared to the dolphins we'd been kicking around.

"What's that *big-ass ugly thing*?!" Soren shouted.

Ryu didn't hesitate. He whipped out his fiery daggers and lunged right at it, fearless.

It fired more blades at him—fast—but he dodged every single one.

"Take cover!" Auri yelled.

But before I could shield anyone, *more* demons emerged. One. Two. A third. A fourth.

Ryu sliced through the first like it was nothing. Then he flipped through the air and landed a blow straight into the second's skull.

Soren squared off with the third, ducking and dodging as it swung its massive, machete-like arms at him.

Maeve was next to me. We looked at each other.

Time to form up.

The battle exploded. Two more demons dropped from the trees. Ryu took them both. Soren kept brawling with the third.

Maeve and I conjured our Veil Ki—our fists glowing. She followed my lead like she'd been doing it her whole life.

You'd think we'd trained together for years.

I punched one demon—it stumbled right into Maeve's attack. She blasted it back with that electric-blue energy of hers, bending its neck sideways with the force.

Her strength was insane.

"That's it!" I shouted, punching again. It collapsed.

She and I both leapt into the air and landed a finishing blow to its chest. It burst open—dead on impact.

We turned to each other—high-fived without even thinking.

But then we turned around...

And the others were gone.

The sky had darkened. The trees were different— *gone.*

"Wait—what just happened?" Maeve asked, spinning around. Her face said it all.

The others were nowhere in sight.

We were alone.

The ground was cold, dark dirt. The trees had vanished. The air stank—like death. Like when we found Travis on the beach.

A thick fog floated above us.

"Maeve..." I said, gripping her arm.

She was shaking a little.

"It's okay. I got you," I said. I was just as freaked out—but I didn't want her to lose her momentum.

We weren't in Starbrook anymore.

Hell, I didn't even know if we were still in the Human World.

A low hum vibrated through the ground.

"There!" I pointed. A huge shadow—looked like a rock formation.

I moved toward it, Maeve close behind.

As we stepped forward, we crunched over bones. They were all sizes.

"Demon bones?" she asked.

We kept walking. The shadow got clearer. It was a cave. A massive one. But that's not what caught my attention.

There was a man sitting outside it.

"Who is that?" I muttered.

He looked familiar. Weirdly familiar.

"He looks... is he hurt? Why is he just sitting there?" Maeve asked, just as confused.

As we got closer, the fog began to clear.

The man looked up.

His smile stretched wide, and his eyes glowed *white*.

I felt Maeve stiffen next to me.

The grin grew wider.

He spoke slowly.

"Perfect. Just as planned."

Chapter Forty
Aurelius

The demons poured out through the darkness.

Soren and Ryu did their best to fend them off. Their screeches rang out from every direction as they charged us in waves. I managed to shield Gwen, narrowly avoiding several blows, while Soren defended Marina—but there were too many of them.

One of them leaped toward her, and she stumbled backward, tripping over the thick roots of a large tree that had burst through the ground.

I heard her cry out—a sharp, broken sound.

Before I could reach her, it was too late.

She fell back, slamming her head against a jagged rock.

Knocked completely unconscious.

"NO—!" Soren roared, so loud it felt like the earth itself trembled.

He grabbed the demon he'd been fighting, put it in a headlock as it scratched and clawed, trying to break free

—then, in a burst of raw rage, *snapped its neck* and hurled the corpse to the ground.

He was seeing red, but still managed to scramble to Marina's side, pulling her into his arms and cradling her tightly against his chest.

"Marina? Wake up! Marina!" he cried out, shaking.

Ryu noticed.

He didn't stop slicing through demons, but his fury spiked. Seeing his sister unconscious lit an even bigger fire in him. His movements turned brutal—relentless.

Black, unnatural blood sprayed everywhere.

"Hmm..." Marina stirred weakly.

"Marina!" Soren held her tighter, one arm around her body, the other cupping the back of her head protectively.

The last demon emerged from the trees, took one look at the massacre of its comrades—Ryu standing over them like death incarnate—and did the one thing we didn't expect:

It ran.

Retreating, fast, back into the woods toward town.

Without a word, Ryu bolted after it.

"What if it's a trap?" Gwen said in a panic. "What if more of them come back?"

I looked at her. "It's time. Time to close the portal."

"But sir!" Gwen protested. "Jude and Maeve—they vanished! What if they're trapped on the other side?"

I knew it was a gamble.

But it was the only way.

If we were successful, maybe... *maybe* one of them would come back.

"Let's set up for the ritual now. While we have the chance," I said.

No demons had returned. The clearing had gone still.

Gwen's hands were shaking as she pulled out her phone. I saw her quickly tap Caelum's name and send a message:

"Find Ryu. Come now."

Soren sat on the ground, still cradling Marina. His lips moved—maybe a prayer. Forehead pressed to hers.

My chest felt hollow.

I felt like a monster.

Like I was blindly following my father's orders instead of making the hard calls myself.

But if I didn't act, more people would die. More lives would be lost. This had to end here.

"Come on. It's time," I said.

We pulled the supplies from the bag—the talisman given to me by King Aurelius. Gwen wiped her eyes.

"Wait—how are we supposed to close it?" she asked. "I thought it needed *their* blood?"

"I don't know," I admitted. "All the books we studied, all the ancient translations—none of it makes sense."

I placed the talisman on the ground. "Get back," I told her.

She stepped behind me.

Soren stayed by Marina, rocking her gently in his arms, just waiting.

I placed my hand over the talisman and poured my royal spirit energy into it. Willing it to activate.

The light burst into the air—bright pastels lighting up

the sky. The power that surged from the talisman knocked us back, the wind howling violently around us.

Then we heard it.

Popping. Booming.

"Fireworks," Gwen said softly.

And I remembered—today was the Fourth of July.

The humans would think the lights and noise were part of a celebration. No one would come investigating. We had a cover, the perfect night for this ritual to take place.

But I still didn't know if Jude and Maeve were alive.

Or how they got pulled into the portal without us.

Whoever was behind this... was watching us.

I focused again.

"*Obcludere*," I commanded the talisman.

The light shifted. The earth groaned. A gravitational pull swept over us—the air felt *heavy*.

Soren shielded Marina as thick branches from nearby trees started crashing down. Gwen braced herself.

It was working.

The ritual required a *sacrifice*—and the seal was lighting up the portal.

Then a blast of light surged ahead of us, traveling ten feet through the forest, carving a path through the shadows.

"That's the portal!" Gwen shouted.

Her hand found mine. She squeezed tight. Tears streamed down her face.

That was where Maeve and Jude had been standing before they vanished.

No demons had come out since.

The ones we fought were already here, hiding, waiting—watching.

"Something pulled them in," Soren said, his voice grim.

Marina stirred weakly. "Marina?" he asked.

"I'm okay—" she whispered. "Where's Maeve?"

There were no words.

The portal had already taken them.

And now, we had no control.

Only one thing could close the seal now.

The death of Jude—

Or the death of Maeve.

The ending had already begun.

Chapter Forty-One
Maeve

The tall man's silhouette became more and more distinct as the fog kept clearing and our vision sharpened. His face... his eyes... they looked like someone I knew. He had long, dark burgundy hair down his back, some of it covering his face. He was skinny, but still muscular. He appeared dirty and wore torn clothing that suggested he had no home to return to—no clothes to change into.

But this place we were in... it was bare. Colorless. Cold. Fog and nothingness stretched in every direction. We couldn't see what was coming toward us.

"This can't be Demon World," I whispered.

The man continued to stare.

"Who the hell are you?" Jude shouted.

He just sat and smiled. Not saying a word since his first comment. Just staring and smiling.

It was chilling. Dark. I could feel his wickedness. He intended to do us harm.

He stood. Even Jude took a step back—but he stood his ground, gritting his teeth.

"Maeve, listen. I think we found who opened the portal... and who's been sending us those demons."

Then, as if on cue, several emerged from the fog and shadows. Big ones. Small ones. These demons slowly walked out.

"Jude, look..." I said. But it was too late. We were already surrounded.

The tall man smiled as they gathered around us. Not attacking. Just... waiting.

"Do you like them?" he finally spoke. "I created them myself."

"What?" I thought. *How?*

"I've been trapped in this hell dimension for over twenty years. And now... I'll break out of here. You two set me free."

I didn't understand. My heart was pounding. The demons were everywhere. There was no way Jude and I could take them all—without our whole team.

Just then, from behind us, a blinding light split the air, tearing it open with a sharp, thunderous crack. The portal lit up—swirling and unstable—its edges sparking wildly as energy rippled outward. A gaping hole of white-hot light hovered in the open space, humming with power. It had been there all along, but we couldn't see it until Aurelius performed the ritual. There was no other explanation.

"Maeve," Jude said in a voice I had never heard from him before. My eyes went wide.

"Maeve. You remember Kayo, right?"

I nodded slowly.

"I'm going to get you out of here. But I need you to do something for me."

I stared at him. He better not be saying what I thought he was saying. No way was I going to try to escape through the portal and leave him. I would never forgive myself.

"I need you to tell her that I love her. More than anything. Please. Make sure she knows."

The man continued smiling at us both.

"You tell her yourself, Jude," I responded firmly.

"Maeve, I'm serious. When you see the chance to leave, I want you out of here. If you escape and I die, it should close the portal. It'll trap him."

"Jude—"

The man stepped forward. The demons around us stirred, like they were ready to pounce.

"You came, just like I knew you would."

The man's smile stretched wider. "Excellent. Thank you, Aurelius."

"Aurelius?" I echoed.

"If it wasn't for your prince, I would have never been able to escape this hellhole I was banished to. Forced to hide and recover, all these years."

The demons growled louder. I got closer to Jude. He stood, bracing himself.

"Not without a fight, Maeve," he said.

I followed his lead and stood tall—even though my legs were shaking.

"Brave and stupid," the man mocked. "These are the Earth's greatest protectors?" He laughed. "No wonder my brother has been able to fool you for so long."

"Brother?" I asked.

"Oh yes. He's there on Earth, walking among you. I was banished here, and him there, in human form. But we will soon continue what we started. Aurelius will pay. Starting with you."

He lunged forward.

Jude threw himself in front of me, blocking the man's attack. The demons got rowdy around us.

"Jude!" I panicked. The man overpowered him.

Jude was pinned to the ground. I tried to run to him but was blasted backwards by the man's energy.

"Stay out of this!" he barked. "And I might let you live."

Jude struggled underneath him.

I looked toward the portal—still there.

"MAEVE! RUN!" Jude screamed. "Go back! Get out of here! MAEVE!"

"Oh no you don't. Attack her!" The man shouted.

Ten demons lunged at once.

"NO!" I screamed, my power bursting out of me—radiating so brightly it formed a shield around my body. The demons screeched as they hit it and disintegrated.

"Oh shit." I hadn't done that in years. The remaining demons fell back.

"Maeve, GO!" Jude shouted again, still trapped. "If you leave, the portal will close!"

"Not so fast," the man growled. He placed his hand on Jude's chest. "Come any closer and I'll kill him!"

I froze.

Then I ran toward him with all the fury I had left, screaming as I summoned a massive blast of energy.

Just like the one Jude and I had conjured together earlier.

"I'm not leaving you, Jude!"

The man effortlessly batted me aside again, extinguishing the blast. I slammed into the ground a few feet away.

He was too strong.

"Now where was I..." He smirked. "See, I can't walk through that portal myself. It would burn me alive. Courtesy of the curse your wretched leader put on me. But now—with your energy—I can disguise myself as you. Leave you both here to die."

"No!" Jude struggled. "Get the fuck off me!"

The man held him tighter.

"You Veilkeepers walked right in. You were the key. But you got it mixed up. I would've never made it out without both of you. I win, AURELIUS."

"AGHHHHHH!" Jude screamed as the man blasted him in the chest. Jude went pale. His body slackened.

"Jude! No!" I cried. "No!"

I tried to stand, but the power was too strong. I couldn't see. I could only hear Jude's cries of pain and the demons screeching.

Then—silence. No more screaming. No Jude.

Just that demonic laughter.

As the light dimmed, my eyes adjusted.

The man was standing.

And Jude's lifeless body lay there, still.

The man ran toward the portal—and leapt through it.

The demons scattered away.

"What...?"

I panicked. I just sat there.

Jude's body wasn't moving.

"Jude…" I whispered. I stood on shaking legs, like a baby deer. "Jude?" I repeated, but nothing. I walked to him slowly.

That beautiful boy who saved me… he was dead.

I dropped to the ground. I couldn't cry—I couldn't breathe. I picked him up and rested his head in my lap.

"Jude…" I whispered.

He wasn't breathing. His eyes—slightly open—were dull. Lifeless.

And the man had escaped.

We were both covered in dirt. Bruised. I could still hear demons in the distance, regrouping maybe. But I didn't care.

I looked at the portal. It was still open but growing smaller. It was closing.

I was the key, but we both were the sacrifice.

The portal believed Jude was still alive and had passed through—since the man stole his life force.

The thing I didn't tell Marina, Auri, and Ryu—not even Jude—was that a small part of me had made peace with dying today. And if given the choice, I would have saved Jude's life all along.

I held him closer.

"Funny," I whispered. "I always thought I'd die alone. At least you're here. Jude… you'll get to see Kayo again."

I channeled everything. Just like Caelum reminded me.

I reached that euphoric state—burning energy radiating off my body.

I held Jude tight. "I promise, my dear friend. Thank you for everything."

The portal would close soon.

I quickly pressed my lips to his—transferring all my life energy into him.

I felt his body start to warm, as mine began to fade. I was cold. So cold.

My life flashed before me.

Running through the Tennessee hills as a child. Becoming a Veilkeeper. Meeting Marina. All the battles. The fans. A stage. Bright lights... fading. Ryu.

I collapsed sideways on top of Jude.

"Go home, Jude," I struggled to say. "Go home... to her."

And then—I was gone.

Chapter Forty-Two
Soren

We waited patiently for one of them to appear. I held my breath, still hoping both Jude and Maeve would come out of the portal glowing in front of us. *Maybe they found a way!* I kept telling myself.

Marina sat in my arms, trembling. I could feel it. She was just as scared as I was. The worst part was, there was nothing either of us could do.

My eyes were starting to burn from staring at the portal's bright, flashing light.

Come on, Jude... I thought.

Then a multicolor flash split through the portal, strobing violently. Someone—or something—was coming through.

Jude? Maeve? Another demon?

Out of the rift stumbled a figure. We saw the silhouette in the flashes. It was a man. My stomach dropped— I didn't recognize him. For a moment, no one moved. Even the air felt like it was holding its breath.

I stood up, ready to defend the group.

"Where's Jude?!" I shouted.

The man grinned, showing black eyes and teeth. His hair was a dark reddish color—almost like Caelum's. That's what stood out to me.

"Dead," the man said.

I couldn't breathe. Jude? Dead? No... It was strange, though. I still felt Jude's energy—but it was only when *this guy* came through the portal.

"You're lying!" I shouted.

The man laughed—bitter and high.

Aurelius stepped forward. "Sin?" he asked, and something about the way he said it made my skin crawl.

"Aw, Prince Aurelius himself," the man said mockingly. "Don't you look dashing. Younger—somehow. What a pleasant surprise for you to come welcome me back. It's been two whole—"

"Decades," Aurelius finished. "What have you done with the two Veilkeepers? Where are they?"

Sin laughed again.

How the hell did Aurelius know this raggedy, dirt-covered clown?

"They wanted to trade places with me. So, they're stuck—where I was banished all those years ago."

"It can't be," Aurelius muttered. "Sin. One of the most ruthless demons to ever haunt the living, the Spirit World, and the Demon World. You were behind all this?"

"Indeed."

"Sir," Gwen said, panicked, "I thought Sin was banished! And if that's true, where is his brother? Where is Sage?"

I didn't know what the hell they were talking about. This was all news to me.

I stepped forward. "I don't give a damn who or what you are. Tell us what you did with our friends, or I'll kill you!"

Sin cackled, louder this time—like a lunatic.

"Stand down, Soren," Aurelius warned, cautious.

"Well, as much as I'd love to stay and chat," Sin said, "I need to go find my brother. It was good seeing you again, Prince Aurelius. Send your father my regards."

He flashed his hand and launched an attack. Aurelius shielded it, blocking it just in time. Sin bolted—in the same direction Ryu had gone earlier, toward the shore.

"Oh, no you don't!" I said, and I took off after him without thinking.

"No, Soren! Come back!" I heard someone shout behind me.

"YOU KILLED MY BEST FRIEND!" I screamed, chasing him with everything I had. He was fast—not human, clearly. I'd seen Caelum and Ryu run like this. Only people like them could match this kind of speed.

We burst out of the woods and onto the beach. I saw Sin in front of me, racing down the shoreline, kicking up sand. Ahead, Ryu was fighting one of those big-ass demons from before—his daggers flashing, sweat and blood in his hair.

Suddenly, another demon leapt from the shadows and tackled me.

"RYU!" I shouted, hoping he'd hear me in time. But before I could even react, I felt something stab into my shoulder—those damn machete-like arms.

"AGHH!" I cried out, the pain making me lose my breath. Blood soaked my shirt.

Then a shadow leapt from my left. Everything blurred. The demon thrashed me around violently—until it didn't. I turned just enough to see Caelum tackle the demon, blasting it straight back to hell with a lethal blow.

"Can you move?" Caelum asked, helping me up.

We watched as Ryu finished his demon too—but Sin was still getting away.

"We can't..." I struggled to speak. "We can't let him get away..."

I broke free from Caelum, ignoring the pain, and ran. Maybe it was adrenaline, but I didn't care. I wasn't letting Sin get away.

"Soren! Wait!" Caelum shouted behind me.

Ryu and I were just catching up when we stopped dead in our tracks. We weren't expecting what we saw next.

A woman—no, a figure—stood glowing in the dark. She had Sin by the throat, lifting him like he weighed nothing. Her clothes looked old and worn, her hair black and stringy, hiding her face. She tossed him around like a rag doll.

"Who is that?" Caelum shouted.

And then it hit me.

That girl—her. From the picture in the restaurant. The one Maeve said she'd seen. *Gladys.*

She held Sin by the neck, her face still hidden. She didn't speak. And the ocean touched my feet—I didn't even realize how close we were to the water. My blood was mixing with the sand.

"Soren, we need to get you help," Caelum growled.

Then Gladys dropped Sin and turned, floating away down the beach. She vanished.

But Sin... who was already weak, was down. Overpowered by a ghost. This was my chance.

Before I died, I'd get at least one hit in.

I ran.

"Soren!" Caelum shouted.

Ryu and Caelum beat me to him—one on each arm, holding him in place.

Sin laughed. "Oh my... I didn't expect to find you so quickly," he said.

"What the hell are you talking about?" I spat up blood. "Shut up!" I shouted, slamming my fist into his face with everything I had. Again. And again. And again.

"YOU KILLED JUDE!" I kept hitting him, until I couldn't see. My vision blurred, my body collapsing.

"SOREN, STOP!" Gwen's voice broke through.

I collapsed backwards into Marina's arms. Her touch — warm. Healing. Her hands trembling as they glowed over my wound.

Gwen dropped to the other side with her first aid kit. Marina's tears were silent, steady. I knew they weren't for me. They were for Maeve.

I laid there in the sand, staring at the stars. I didn't notice them before. The clouds had finally cleared. Fireworks boomed in the distance.

"I'm not from this part of the world," I whispered. "But I think they call today Independence Day..."

How fitting. This would be when you'd go, Jude.

Jude had been part of my life since I could remember.

Brothers from different mothers. I don't remember a day without him.

He always loved fireworks. Too bad this is how I'll always remember them now.

I thought beating the hell out of Sin would make me feel better. But it didn't. I didn't feel anything. Not even Marina's hand in mine.

Because my best friend was dead.

Aurelius stepped forward to Sin, who was still being held between Ryu and Caelum. I sat up as much as I could to watch.

He was calm. Quiet. Controlled. He reached for Sin's wrist, his fingers glowing. He whispered something in an ancient tongue—and glowing chains wrapped around Sin, snapping tight.

Sin laughed weakly. "Brother... how could you let them do this...?"

Then a black obsidian box formed around him. Engulfing him as the chains wrapped around him tighter and he began to shrink into the box. Magic sealed it tight. The box fell to the sand with a dull thud.

And then the light vanished.

Gwen picked up the box. Pale. Furious.

"Teleport," Aurelius ordered. "Take him to Spirit World Prison. Don't wait."

Gwen hesitated—but nodded.

"I'll try to recover our Veilkeepers' bodies," Aurelius said. "Let me know if their souls are already there."

She wiped her face and vanished.

I collapsed again, laying back on the sand. The ocean licked my arm, pulling back.

I could've died right there. Knowing he was gone.

After Gwen vanished, everyone was quiet. All of us stared out at the sea. The waves rolled in. Soft. Endless.

"There's no way to find them, is there?" I asked. Eyes wet. Voice cracked.

No one answered.

Because there wasn't.

Chapter Forty-Three
Jude

There was just darkness. Cold darkness—then breath.

I gasped, my body lunging upright, coughing as the sudden rush of sharp air hit my lungs, burning them like I'd been underwater for hours. I took deep breaths, looking around, trying to remember—trying to recall what happened. It all started to come back to me, like waking up in the morning.

I was alive. Strong. Fully restored.

I didn't understand—until I looked down into my lap.

"Maeve..."

She lay across me, completely still and limp.

"Maeve?" My voice cracked. My eyes started to burn uncontrollably, like a really bad allergy attack. I knew what this was, but I wasn't ready to accept it. I shook her.

"MAEVE! WAKE UP!" I said, still shaking her. Nothing.

I looked over to see the portal, still closing—slowly. It was smaller, still bright. Maybe half my size now, but it wouldn't be long. If I didn't go through, it would close, and I'd be stuck here forever.

I pushed up onto my elbows and cradled her in my arms, brushing her golden hair away from her beautiful face. No response. Not a sign of life left in her. Her skin was paler than usual, her lips parted as if her last breath had been stolen away.

"No... no, no, no." I squeezed her tightly, rocking back and forth. The burning in my eyes evolved into full-formed tears, like drops of fire running down my face.

The realization hit me like a hammer.

She died for me. The power I was feeling inside—this strength—it was Maeve's.

She gave everything. For me. All that she had left, just so I could come back. And now, she was gone. I did this to her. I did this... to my friend.

Maeve really was a Veilkeeper. True-hearted, strong, and loyal in the end. She gave up her life to save me—her arrogant, asshole teammate who didn't deserve to be saved.

The tears blurred my vision, hot and angry as they fell onto her face. I held her tighter, clinging to her like I could anchor her back to life through sheer desperation.

It was no use.

"I'm sorry," I choked out. My voice shook as grief strangled me.

"You weren't useless, Maeve. You were never useless. You're the bravest person I know. The nicest. You sacrificed yourself for the world... for me. You are the strongest Veilkeeper."

I pressed my forehead to the side of her head. My

wet, heavy tears fell into her hair. I closed my eyes, but it was no use. The tears kept coming. I couldn't stop crying.

"I was wrong about you," I whispered. "So wrong. You were always my friend. Please come back to me. Please... please..."

The world didn't answer.

Instead, the shadows stirred around us. They were back. I heard them—low growls, claws scraping against stone. Demons creeping closer, sensing weakness. Eager for an easy kill.

I didn't move. I didn't want to. I felt strong enough to fight them, but what was the use? Maeve was gone. I couldn't. I couldn't put her down. I kept holding her, eyes shut tight.

"It's not fair," I muttered bitterly. "I got to live, and you died. Why? It's not right. It's not— it was supposed to be me. I didn't protect you. It was my one job, and I didn't—"

The growls grew louder. They were surrounding us now. My fingers tightened around Maeve's limp hand.

"Go ahead," I whispered to them, brokenly. "Kill me too. I don't care. I don't deserve to live if she had to die."

I looked at the portal. It was half the size it was before, starting to close faster now. I closed my eyes in defeat. Only a living being could travel between dimensions. The portal would reject her even if I tried to take her back with me. And if I jumped through and left her body here—to be eaten and ripped to shreds by demons— I'd never forgive myself.

I won't go back without her.

"Go on," I said to the monsters. "Do it." I held her tight. "Maeve... I'll see you soon."

The shadows pounced. I flinched.

But then—the strangest thing. They never reached us.

A sudden, unexplainable warmth ignited beneath my hands where I held Maeve. It wasn't Veil energy. A kind I'd never felt before—foreign, pure.

I blinked, confused—then gasped as a radiant teal light, the same color as Maeve's eyes, erupted from her body.

"Maeve—?"

Her chest glowed. Her hair lifted gently, caught in a nonexistent breeze. Her limbs floated weightless. Her eyes shot open—brilliant, glowing like twin stars.

The demons screeched—not in anger, but in terror. They tried to retreat.

Maeve's light swelled—huge, consuming. It exploded outward in a wave so intense, so pure and controlled, that the creatures disintegrated instantly. Ash scattered like dust.

I stared, stunned, as the portal overhead reacted violently to the surge of power. It shook. I thought it was going to collapse.

I scooted backward, letting her go as her body rose into the air, still surrounded by blinding light. My hair blew wildly in the wind she was emitting. I tried to stand but was in awe.

Her light reached the portal like a lance, stretching and tearing it open.

I looked back at Maeve. She didn't say a word. Her

eyes met mine—and in that gaze, she didn't look like herself anymore. I saw someone—*something* else. A power that wasn't Moonveil. Ancient. Otherworldly. Beautiful.

I wasn't sure if she was still Maeve.

Then she smiled at me and reached out her hand.

I hesitated—then took it.

I was lifted off the ground before I could think. Before I could speak, the light engulfed us both.

I felt myself rise, as though gravity no longer mattered. The world spun and broke apart around us. All I remember is flashes of light. We flew through the portal, carried by an unseen force. It looked like we were inside a kaleidoscope. My stomach twisted like I was on a roller-coaster. Once we were out on the other side, back in our world, I looked down—and realized that even though we were still mid-air, we were back in the human world. I saw the portal in the woods below us collapse. The seal worked its magic, and with a thunderous crack heard around the world, it sealed forever.

The demons were gone.

Only the light around Maeve and me remained.

We floated in the sky. I looked at her—really looked. She stared back.

This time... she was *her*. She was Maeve.

"Maeve!" I shouted, overwhelmed, as I hugged her so tight I could've broken something. I clung to her, shaking. She held onto me too. I pulled back—we were floating, still flying, but starting to descend. Her eyes dimmed, the glow fading... but she was *alive*.

Breathing. Real.

As we broke through the trees, I looked down toward the beach. The others—Soren, Auri, Ryu, Caelum, Marina—they were running below, following our light, trying to catch up to wherever we'd land. We hovered over the ocean. I knew we'd drop soon.

"Hold on!" I said, gripping her tight. And then...
SPLASH!

We hit the water. Cold waves closed over us instantly. I lost my grip on Maeve—for just a second. My heart pounded as I pulled her back, refusing to let go this time. I pushed her above the surface. The waves had calmed. Like they knew we were there. But then I realized it was Marina manipulating them in our favor. Making it easier for us to swim to shore.

We surfaced just in time, coughing but both of us were okay.

I held her arms as we floated in front of each other, face to face, both in shock. What the hell had just happened?

We floated in the ocean while the night sky above us exploded with fireworks. Everything else settled, except the bright colors bursting overhead—like even the rest of the world knew to celebrate what we just did.

The water rocked us gently, soft waves lapping our shoulders. The world went quiet. We heard the others calling from shore. We weren't far out. Our heads bobbed in the water. We started swimming back slowly.

Then Maeve stopped.

I turned around, not leaving her. The water was waist-deep now. We could stand.

She just stared at the fireworks.

"Maeve," I said, grabbing her arm, gently pulling her closer. I stood beside her, watching reds, blues, and golds explode like dreams across the sky.

Then she made a sound. I thought she was crying, but... she was laughing.

She finally said, "How embarrassing—" then kept laughing. Louder. "How embarrassing would it be if we survived all that, only to get eaten by a shark?"

I stared at her, stunned—*that* was the first thing she said?

But then it hit me—I started laughing too.

We laughed, and laughed, and we didn't know why. It wasn't just the joke. It was everything. We both *died*, and now we were somehow alive again, standing in the ocean watching fireworks.

We were hysterical. We'd lost it. And it was perfect.

The wind shifted. Clouds rolled in. Then—out of nowhere—light rain began. Soft at first, then steadier. It didn't stop. We looked at each other—and laughed even harder. Of course it would pour rain on us.

We could hear the others shouting, closer now. I looked down at Maeve and saw her laughter turn to tears.

She broke down. Tears of joy, I think—so over-whelmed. She cried into my chest. I held her, the rain falling on us both. I looked up at the last fireworks blazing in the sky—aggressive, defiant, determined to keep going despite the rain.

As the show ended, we turned and walked toward the sand.

Soren and Marina ran toward us. Marina tackled Maeve, holding her tightly. Maeve hugged her back.

Next thing I knew, I was being lifted off the ground by my freakishly tall best friend.

"Easy, man!" I laughed.

"Jude, you're alive! You did it!" Soren cheered.

The others all stared, stunned and relieved.

I looked at Auri. He turned away.

"Sorry," he said. "Sand in my eyes again." A lie. His eyes were red.

I then looked at Maeve.

I nodded. "It's over."

She nodded back and smiled— face flushed, hair soaked.

Ryu walked up and draped his cloak over her shoulders.

I turned to Soren, who was already pulling me into another one of his signature brotherly bear hugs. This time, I didn't push him away. I hugged him back and said, "Let's go home, man."

Chapter Forty-Four
Aurelius

The air in the Spirit World was always unnerving and still, but it felt worse upon my return. Gwen had successfully managed to bring back Sin, a demon who had been on our most-wanted list for over twenty years. Still, so many questions remained.

He was weak—he'd been hiding in the dimension our Veilkeepers had successfully closed off. But how? How was Sin able to create and open a portal? An invisible one at that.

It would explain why he was so weak, why he couldn't get through himself—but the other demons could.

My theory was that creating and opening the portal itself had drained his energy, so then he borrowed Jude's—disguising himself and crossing dimensions, causing the seal to almost close the portal, trapping our Veilkeepers forever.

Sin got lucky, escaping the demon dimension—but not lucky enough. Now, he was being held prisoner here in the Spirit World, where he belonged. Long overdue. However, there was one problem: if Sin was here... where was his brother, Sage?

Gwen and I stood in front of the prison, watching Sin sit with his head down, hair hanging in his face. The spirit workers slammed the door shut behind him. Sealed tightly by cold, heavy walls and incantations that held him inside.

"It's funny," I said to Gwen, as we stared into his cell. "For years, we searched for the brothers—Sin and Sage. Not a peep. A lot of people here and even in the Demon World believed the two had died. But I never thought we'd find one without the other."

"Yes," Gwen said. "All the crimes they committed back then... horrific. Brutal. Gave Kosei the fight of his life. He was way in over his head."

"Yeah. And he was our only Veilkeeper at the time," I reminded her.

"Do you think Sage is really hiding in the Human World like he told Jude and Maeve?" she asked.

"I don't know. But wherever he is... I have a feeling he's going to reveal himself soon—especially once he catches word that we captured his brother."

"He's a wanted man. Surely, he won't expose his hiding spot. Sin's hopeless now. He's caught."

I shook my head. "No. Those two are thick as thieves. Everything they did—every crime they committed—they were always in it together. I don't believe this time is any different."

Gwen nodded slowly.

"Well, our work here is done. I have to give my final report. Wish me luck," I said, turning away.

"Good luck, sir," she said with a smile.

I placed my hand on her shoulder, patting it gently before walking off.

The cold marble floors reflected the pale pink sky overhead. After a long walk down endless corridors and climbing the stone stairs, I reached the giant doors of my father's chamber. I knocked, and one of the guards let me in without a word.

Inside, my father stood by the large glass windows, overlooking the Spirit World. Today, the clouds and mist fogged much of the view.

He turned slightly, just enough to acknowledge me, then stared back out the window.

"It's done," I said simply, bowing my head. "The threat is contained. The Veilkeepers are safe. They're already returning home, as well as the others. It's over."

My father—a large man with a long black beard that swayed as he turned—met my eyes with his golden gaze. It didn't soften.

"I don't buy it," he said.

My fists curled at my sides. I took a breath, exhaling through my nose.

"With respect, Father, the portal is sealed. The demons were eradicated. Sin is in captivity and will finally be formally tried for his past and present crimes. There's nothing left to—"

"This is only the beginning," he interrupted coldly. His voice echoed through the chamber, final and absolute. "Sin will stand trial, but we mustn't forget—Sage is still out there. And I will not turn a blind eye to what happened tonight." He paused, eyes narrowing at me. "It raises questions. Dangerous ones."

He waved a hand, dismissing the guards. That alone was unusual.

"Leave us. I need to speak to my son alone."

The guards exited without a sound. Once the doors closed, I turned my attention back to him.

He walked toward the table near his desk. On it sat Sin's containment cube—the very one we used to capture and transport him here. It still pulsed faintly.

My father stared at it, not at me.

"Tell me, my son," he said sharply. "Why wasn't the portal simply closed? How did Sin make it into the world of the living in the first place? You know as well as I do—if the spell had been performed the way it was supposed to be, then the portal would have been sealed long before Sin had the time to escape."

I kept my face composed, though unease twisted in my stomach.

"I don't know," I answered truthfully. I only knew what the Veilkeepers told me of what transpired in that dimension. My father had already been briefed, and even then—he still had questions.

"Sin mentioned his brother is in the Human World," I added. "But the whereabouts of Sage are still unknown."

My father was quiet. His lips pursed.

"If Sage was with Sin that night... and they both managed to cross over..." His voice lowered darkly. "It would have been catastrophic. You know nothing of that realm, do you? Sage could be hiding there."

"No," I said slowly. "Father, forgive me—but this is the first I'm hearing about multiple dimensions. I thought there was only one—the one we've documented."

He curled his lip, unimpressed.

"Son, there are many worlds. Many realities. Not all demons belong to the same hell you were taught about. Dimensions were never meant to cross—that's what made this so dangerous. Sin was stranded in another realm entirely. That's why we couldn't locate him for decades. He used what strength he'd built up over twenty years to tear through the fabric of reality and re-enter ours. That's why he was so weak. But still strong enough to challenge our Veilkeepers."

He turned back toward the window. The clouds had begun to move.

"He will be interrogated. And when I'm satisfied with what I know, he will then be executed. No more chances. I cannot risk a being who has summoned power similar to that of a god to exist in the human, demon, or spirit worlds. Even in captivity."

"That's too kind," I muttered, my voice tight with anger. Death would be ideal for Sin. He'd gladly accept it. I wanted him tormented—for eternity. "He risked *everything!*" I shouted. "The Veilkeepers! Innocent lives! The lives of the others on my team!"

My father's gaze darkened. He leaned forward.

"Careful, Prince Aurelius," he warned. "Do you want to end up like your sister?"

"No, sir," I said, clenching my fists, gritting my teeth. Looking down.

The words struck like venom. I bit down so hard it ached.

I said nothing—not because I agreed, but because arguing with him would change nothing.

He smiled, satisfied with my obedience and silence. Then his tone shifted.

"And yet... there is still something else troubling me."

I stayed quiet, waiting.

"Maeve," he said bluntly. "What transpired with her was not ordinary. I trust you know that. That was no Veilkeeper power. It was trained. Tempered. Raw and far too powerful. If something like that ever lost control..."

I stiffened.

"Her power disrupted the portal. Erased the demons. That wasn't normal. That wasn't Moonveil energy," he continued, voice low—curious, almost like he was observing a new weapon.

He stood, and his tone grew icier with each word.

"She will need to be watched. Carefully. Very closely. I trust *you* will do that."

He turned to me. The way he stared—cold, calculating—wasn't just concern. It was a threat.

His words hung in the air, heavy and sharp.

"Yes, Father," I said, trying not to scowl.

He smiled and turned back to the window, breaking the weight of his golden glare.

"That is all. You're dismissed."

I bowed, turning on my heel before he could see the

storm in my expression. But as I walked away, his words replayed in my mind.

She will need to be watched... carefully... closely...

He wasn't intrigued by Maeve's power.

He wasn't grateful she'd saved the Human World.

He wasn't proud.

He was calculating her. Studying her. And something told me that whatever he was planning...

There wasn't going to be any mercy.

Chapter Forty-Five
Maeve

We all stood outside the Hummingbird Inn one final time with our bags packed. The early morning sun was warm, and salt air was carried on a slight breeze. It was a beautiful day here—but I was ready to leave. Where was I going? Who knows. But I was over being near the beach.

I pulled my baseball cap down low as people walked by, smiling. They were admiring the workers finally rebuilding and repairing the front entrance to the inn.

As the innocent townspeople moved through the streets, you'd never guess that the ordeal we went through the night before had even happened.

It was the first pleasant day in a long time. I guess things were back to normal here now that the portal was closed. There wasn't a dark, heavy cloud hanging over this small coastal town anymore. Things had finally settled.

Mission completed. It felt like time to leave.

All of us stood outside the inn with our bags, waiting for our separate vans that would take us where we needed to go. Jude and the guys had a van coming to take them to the airport. Marina and I couldn't risk flying or being seen, so we were taking a van all the way down from the tip of the East Coast back toward New York. It would be a long ride, but like I said—I was ready to leave.

What I *wasn't* ready for was saying goodbye. Especially to Ryu... and of course, Jude.

I hugged Soren and Caelum, careful with my injuries. We were all still pretty banged up. Marina hugged Soren too, but he wouldn't let her go.

"Promise we'll see each other soon!" he said, engulfing her in one of his famous bear hugs.

"I promise!" she laughed, squeezing him back.

When I got to Jude, I hesitated for just a second before wrapping my arms around him. He did the same.

"Guess this is it for now," I said, still hugging him.

"Bummer," he replied, his chin resting on top of my head.

"My parents are expecting me to check in, so I'm headed back," I said, pulling back just slightly to look up at him, our arms still around each other. "But who knows... maybe we'll find ourselves in your little corner of the world. I'd love to meet Kayo and Kosei."

Jude smiled back. "I'm counting on it."

Two white vans pulled up in front of the inn at the same time. The townsfolk watched as Soren and Caelum started loading our things, and Jude went over to help with theirs.

Ryu walked over to assist, but I stepped in front of him, blocking his way. Around my waist, I still had his cloak from last night, the one he'd lent me.

"Here," I said untying it. "I never got the chance to thank you."

He smiled. "You keep it," he said. "I have so many."

"Are you sure?" I asked. "I already have your other clothes from the other night too…"

He shrugged, still smiling. "I'm sure. Something to remember me by."

"Like I could ever forget."

"Maeve! We're ready," Marina called out—not impatiently, but the driver was probably eager to go.

I looked at Ryu and, without warning, threw my arms around him. His breath hitched—maybe he hadn't expected it—but then I felt him hug me back, loosely but warm. I didn't torture him long. I pulled away quickly—but not before sneaking a fast kiss right on his left cheek.

Then I turned and scurried toward the van, my face burning red. I climbed into the back with Marina. Soren, ever the gentleman, shut the door behind me. I waved at him, but my eyes were on Ryu, still standing there, staring at me—wonderstruck.

I waved at him through the glass.

He slowly raised his hand and smiled.

I turned to Marina, who was already giggling. She'd seen the whole thing.

"Oh, Maeve… what am I going to do with you?" she joked.

Our van was in front of the boy's van. We were loaded and ready to go. Slowly, we pulled away.

I turned around in my seat, watching the guys gather by their van—Ryu climbing in, Caelum laughing as Jude and Soren shoved each other around, arguing over who was getting in first or who got the front seat.

They became smaller and smaller as we drove away.

Marina put in her headphones and closed her eyes.

I watched the town pass by—small businesses opening their doors for another day in Starbrook. The ocean sparkled to Marina's side of the van. Trees blurred past on mine. The farther we drove, the quieter it felt.

No longer in town, but not yet at the city line.

And then—out of the corner of my eye—something caught the light. A figure.

I thought my mind was playing tricks on me, but there, standing just beyond the tree line... was a girl.

Long dark hair rippling in the breeze. A pale nightgown that fluttered like silk. Her skin glowed in the sunlight, and her face was—peaceful. Smiling.

She lifted her hand as if she was waving.

I could've sworn she was looking straight at me.

My stomach turned cold.

"Marina!" I whispered urgently, elbowing her gently. "Look!" I said, turning in my seat.

Marina sat up and peered out the window, looking back.

"What? I don't see anything," she said.

I turned again.

The girl was gone. Just trees and morning haze.

I stared a moment longer, heart thudding, but didn't panic.

Then I shook my head and leaned back against the seat.

"I'm losing it," I muttered, trying to brush off the chill. But I knew who she was.

Thank you, Gladys. I smiled to myself as we crossed the city line officially out of Starbrook.

I sat for a while, replaying the mission over and over in my mind—from start to finish. Deep down, I knew in ways none of us yet understood, this wasn't the end.

Not for them.

Not for us.

And not for me.

All I could think about was seeing the others again.

I kept my eyes on the road ahead. Somewhere between sadness that we had to say goodbye, and excitement for what was to come next.

Follow and Subscribe:

TikTok: @cozy_lofi_dreams

YouTube: @CozyLofiDreams

Instagram: @kristenjadeling

About the Author

My name is Kristen Ling, and the *Moonveil Saga* has lived in my imagination for years. I used to play out the story at night before falling asleep, during the day while drifting off in class, and even in my subconscious while dreaming.

Each character holds a special place in my heart. I designed them with care, hoping others would come to love them as much as I do.

Now, these stories are no longer just mine — they're yours too. That's a little scary, but more than anything, I'm grateful you chose to read them.

Thank you for being here. I hope you enjoy this novel as much as I've loved creating it.